Beyond Reasonable Doubt

A Play

Jeffrey Archer

Samuel French - London
New York - Toronto - Hollywood

BEYOND REASONABLE DOUBT

The first London production of *Beyond Reasonable Doubt* was presented by Lee Menzies, at the Queens Theatre on 22nd September, 1987, with the following cast of characters:

Court Usher	Brian Ellis
Clerk of the Court	Peter Clapham
Mr Justice Tredwell	Andrew Cruickshank
Anthony Blair-Booth QC	Jeffry Wickham
Det. Chief Inspector Travers	David Weston
Sir David Metcalfe QC	Frank Finlay
Prison Officer	Liam Kennedy
Mrs Rogers	Antonia Pemberton
Dr Weeden	Robert James
Lionel Hamilton	David Langton
Mr Cole (Junior Counsel for the Crown)	Daniel Davies
Robert Pierson (Junior Counsel with Sir David)	Philip York
Stenographer	Angela Ellis
Lady Metcalfe	Wendy Craig

Directed by David Gilmore
Designed by Tim Goodchild
Lighting by Mark Henderson

Company Stage Manager   Peter Gardner
Deputy Stage Manager   Michael Towner
Assistant Stage Managers   Penelope Foxley, Donna Percival

The action of the play takes place in the Central Criminal Court (The Old Bailey) and in the home of Sir David and Lady Metcalfe in Wimbledon

Time—the present

SYNOPSIS OF SCENES

IMPORTANT NOTICE

It is a condition of the licence agreement for productions of BEYOND REASONABLE DOUBT that no changes whatsoever are made in the text.

The author of the play must be credited in all programmes distributed in connection with performances of the play. In all instances in which the title of the play appears for the purposes of advertising, publicizing or otherwise exploiting the play the name of the author must appear on a separate line, on which no other matter appears, immediately following the title of the play.

ACT I

The Trial

The Central Criminal Court—The Old Bailey. Morning

In court are the Usher, the Clerk, Anthony Blair-Booth QC, Robert Pierson, the Prison Officer, Sir David Metcalfe, Cole and the Stenographer

Usher Be upstanding in court.

All rise

The Judge enters

All persons who have anything to do before my lords, the Queen's Justices, at the Central Criminal Court, draw near and give your attendance. God Save the Queen.

All bow and the Judge returns the bow. Everyone sits and Sir David takes his place in the dock

Clerk (*to the jury i.e. the audience*) Members of the jury. The defendant, Sir David Metcalfe, Knight, stands charged with one count of murder. To this count, he has pleaded "not guilty". Your charge therefore is to hearken unto the evidence and say whether he be guilty or no.

Judge (*to the audience*) Ladies and gentlemen, each one of you is now a member of the jury whose solemn task it is to try Sir David Metcalfe for murder. This case has already attracted much lurid publicity, but as you embark upon your labours you must put all such matters from your mind. You have sworn to give a true verdict according to the evidence. The only evidence that matters is the evidence heard in this court. When you return home your family and friends are bound to ask what you have been doing at the Old Bailey. If you mention this case they will not only ask you for your views upon it, they will give you theirs. But they have taken no jury oath, they have heard no evidence. In my experience it is always those who have never been in court who are most certain as to what the verdict should be. The springs of justice flow from knowledge not ignorance. So please do not talk to anyone about this case and don't allow anyone to talk to you. It is you and you alone who will decide if Sir David Metcalfe is guilty or not guilty of murder. Yes, Mr Blair-Booth.

Blair-Booth rises, bows, very slightly

Blair-Booth May it please your lordship, members of the jury . . . in this case I appear for the Crown, together with my learned friend, Mr Cole. The defendant, Sir David Metcalfe, QC, has elected to represent himself. With the leave of his lordship, Sir David is assisted by my learned friend Mr Pierson. Members of the jury, the Crown will not dwell overlong on its opening address, for I feel certain that you will find this case a simple one.

The Judge promptly intervenes

Judge I shall be most interested to follow your argument, Mr Blair-Booth. In more than forty years' involvement with the law, I've yet to come across a simple case.

Blair-Booth If it so please your lordship. Members of the jury, you will find that there is only one count on the indictment—that of murder. The deliberate, non-accidental cold killing of Lady Millicent Metcalfe by the defendant her husband, Sir David Metcalfe. Members of the jury, it gives me no pleasure to appear for the Crown on this occasion. Sir David has had such a distinguished legal career that I am sure you are aware he was an ornament of the Bar. Indeed Chairman of the Bar Council. So you will appreciate how distressing it is for me to find myself prosecuting a former colleague. I have not avoided that grave responsibility, realizing that no man can be above the law and that justice must always be seen to be done. The Crown will present a case which will convince you, members of the jury, beyond reasonable doubt, that Sir David Metcalfe did wilfully murder his wife in the early hours of March twenty-fourth this year. The Crown will also show that the relationship between Sir David and Lady Metcalfe was not a happy one and had, in the period preceding her death, become acrimonious. Earlier in the evening in question, the two of them had quarrelled noisily and openly and later, when the opportunity to poison Lady Metcalfe presented itself so conveniently, Sir David grasped at the chance to be rid of his loyal and devoted wife. The Crown will further show how he went about this evil task, deliberately and knowingly administering the wrong medicine to Lady Metcalfe, thus giving her a lethal overdose of the drug, Cyclotoxelix. The Crown will call witnesses to show a clear motive for this calculated murder and, most important of all, a witness to the murder itself. The Crown will leave no room for doubt about the actions taken by Sir David Metcalfe in the early hours of that fatal March morning, and you will, we submit, be left with no alternative but to find Sir David guilty, unhappy and unpalatable though that may be. My lord, we call our first witness, Inspector Travers.

The Prison Officer stands and announces Inspector Travers, as he will do for all other witnesses, from the lobby outside the double doors. He then shuts the doors and returns to his seat and whatever book he may be reading

The Inspector enters. Whenever he addresses the jury he looks straight at the audience. All witnesses do this in order to make the audience feel they are the jury

Usher Take the testament in your right hand and read from the card.
Travers I swear by Almighty God that the evidence I shall give shall be the truth, the whole truth and nothing but the truth.

Blair-Booth Is your name Richard William Travers and are you a Detective Chief Inspector with the Serious Crime Squad?

Travers Yes, sir.

Blair-Booth On the twenty-fourth of March last when Lady Metcalfe was killed——

Sir David Objection, my lord.

Blair-Booth I apologize, my lord. I should have said, "died".

Sir David Though it was never your intention to do so.

Blair-Booth Inspector, you, I think can produce a copy of the death certificate. My lord, it is an agreed document in the jury bundle. Under the heading, "Cause of Death", what do we read, Inspector?

Travers The certificate states natural causes, my lord, and then the word "Lymphosarcoma".

Blair-Booth At the time, did you have any good reason to doubt the accuracy of the certificate?

Travers No, sir.

Blair-Booth No-one came forward to suggest that this death might have been other than the result of natural causes?

Travers No, sir.

Blair-Booth Sir David Metcalfe never made any effort to contact you in particular or the police generally?

Travers No, sir.

Blair-Booth Then what first aroused your suspicions, Inspector?

Travers The appearance at Wimbledon Police Station of Lady Metcalfe's housekeeper, Mrs Eileen Rogers.

Blair-Booth Did she make a written statement on that occasion?

Travers Yes, sir.

Blair-Booth What was the substance of that statement?

Travers She stated that she had witnessed Sir David Metcalfe poison his wife in the early hours of March twenty-fourth. She claimed that she had clearly seen him administer a fatal dose of Cyclotoxelix even though he must have known that Lady Metcalfe had taken a similar dose only a few hours earlier. She said she'd watched him put it in a cup of tea.

Blair-Booth What course of action did you take once you had learned this piece of information, Inspector?

Travers We obtained an exhumation order to remove the body from Wimbledon cemetery.

Blair-Booth And was that order carried out?

Travers Yes, sir. (*Reading from his notes*) The senior pathologist at the Home Office, Sir James Buckley, confirmed there was a far higher amount of Cyclotoxelix in the body than was consistent with the normal weekly dosage.

Blair-Booth My lord, the pathologist's report is agreed and is in the jury's bundle of documents. When the overdose had been confirmed by the Home Office pathologist what action did you take?

Travers I interviewed … (*checking his notes*) … Dr John Weeden, Lady Metcalfe's doctor; Mrs Rogers, the housekeeper; and Sir David himself. I then made my report and sent it to the Director of Public Prosecutions.

Blair-Booth Yes. And if you had such a clear indication that Sir David himself might have been involved in poisoning his wife, why did you not arrest him immediately?

Travers I did not consider it prudent, sir, to arrest the Chairman of the Bar Council on a charge of murder without the authority of the DPP.

Blair-Booth Quite so, Inspector. One would not wish to arrest someone of such eminence as Sir David Metcalfe unless one was absolutely certain of one's ground——

Sir David Objection, my lord. This sort of comment is quite improper and also prejudiced although not untypical.

Judge Yes, Mr Blair-Booth, you must avoid trying to be both Judge and Jury, as well as Prosecuting Counsel. It is a convenient but undesirable trinity.

Blair-Booth I apologize, my lord. I merely wanted the jury to realize the care and forbearance shown by the Inspector before he considered arresting Sir David. Could you tell the jury what happened next, Inspector?

Travers I obtained a warrant for the arrest of Sir David Metcalfe. Which I executed on the afternoon of April eleventh . . . (*he checks his notes*) . . . at his home in Wimbledon. I charged him with the murder of his wife, Lady Metcalfe.

Blair-Booth When you arrested Sir David, Inspector, how did he react?

Travers He seemed—distraught.

Blair-Booth He seemed distraught. Did he say anything?

Travers He volunteered no statement, sir.

Blair-Booth He volunteered no statement when being arrested for the murder of his wife?

Travers No, sir.

Blair-Booth Thank you, Inspector. (*He sits down*)

Judge Do you wish to cross-examine this witness, Sir David?

Sir David I do, my lord. Inspector, when making an arrest is it not your duty to inform the accused person that he need not make a statement?

Travers Yes, sir.

Sir David Did you in my case?

Travers No, sir.

Sir David Why not?

Travers It seemed superfluous with one of the leading legal authorities in the land and indeed proved so.

Sir David However, you did not carry out the recommended Home Office procedure.

Travers No, sir.

Sir David Inspector, if I had killed my wife in the manner indicated by the Crown, surely I could have destroyed the evidence quite simply by having her body cremated?

Travers Most criminals think they're cleverer than the law. That's usually how we catch them.

Sir David You told the court I looked distraught when you arrested me. Could this not have been a reaction to the recent death of my wife and all the *unnecessary* unpleasantness that had surrounded the post-mortem?

Travers I can't say, sir. It was some weeks after the event.

Sir David The "event"? Some weeks after? Queen Victoria remained distressed for forty years after the death of her husband, Inspector. No further questions, my lord.

Judge Inspector, did Sir David seem distressed before you told him you were going to arrest him?

Travers Difficult to say, my lord. I was so nervous at the thought of going to arrest the Chairman of the Bar Council, I just put the charge to him as soon as I walked through the door.

Judge Um, I see. Thank you, Inspector. Your next witness, Mr Blair-Booth.

Blair-Booth My lord, I should like to call Mrs Eileen Rogers.

Mrs Rogers enters

Usher Please take the testament in your right hand and read from the card.

Mrs Rogers I swear by Almighty God that the evidence I shall give shall be the truth, the whole truth and nothing but the truth.

Judge Would you like to be seated, Mrs Rogers?

Mrs Rogers Thank you, no. I'll stand.

Judge As you wish.

Blair-Booth Is your name Eileen Rogers?

Mrs Rogers Yes, it is.

Blair-Booth Where do you live?

Mrs Rogers (*softly*) Do I have to tell you, with him here? (*She points to Sir David*)

Judge Could you speak up, Mrs Rogers?

Mrs Rogers Do I have to tell you with him here?

Blair-Booth No I don't think that will be necessary, but did you previously live at forty-four The Oaks, Wimbledon, the home of the late Lady Metcalfe?

Mrs Rogers Yes, I did.

Judge Would you please address your replies to the jury, Mrs Rogers?

Blair-Booth And were you in the former employ of Sir David and Lady Metcalfe as housekeeper and general help?

Mrs Rogers Yes. I worked for Lady Metcalfe for over seven years and lived in the house for nearly three, ever since my husband deserted me, but I have since left to take up employment elsewhere.

Blair-Booth Understandably. Mrs Rogers, I should like to start by going over what you remember of the evening of March twenty-third, from the moment Sir David arrived home.

Mrs Rogers Yes, my lord.

Blair-Booth No, you call me "sir" and his lordship, "my lord".

Mrs Rogers Yes, sir.

Blair-Booth Did Sir David arrive home late or early that night?

Mrs Rogers Late. He was nearly always late.

Blair-Booth Did this cause any unpleasantness between Sir David and Lady Metcalfe?

Mrs Rogers Not from Lady Metcalfe, but Sir David can always pick a quarrel over the slightest thing, especially when he's in one of his moods.

Sir David My lord, I must object. This is quite absurd——
Judge (*interrupting him*) You will have your chance to cross-examine, Sir David, as you well know.
Blair-Booth So, Sir David did arrive home late, and Lady Metcalfe seemed distressed by this.
Mrs Rogers Yes. She told him he was a drunk and that alcohol would destroy his brain.
Blair-Booth And what was his reply to that?
Mrs Rogers He became angry. He shouted at her. He said, "You will regret those words, woman." And then he hit her.
Blair-Booth Hit her? You actually saw him hit her?
Mrs Rogers No, sir, but I heard her plead with him not to hit her again.
Blair-Booth And then what happened?
Mrs Rogers I tried to think of some excuse to get back into the drawing-room.
Blair-Booth And did you?
Mrs Rogers Yes. I made Lady Metcalfe a cup of coffee and went in early to give her her pills.
Blair-Booth Yes, we'll come to that in a moment. Let me ask you, Mrs Rogers, did Sir David drink a lot that night?
Mrs Rogers His breath smelt of alcohol when he came home, then he drank a bottle of wine and later another bottle. I know because I cleared them away.
Blair-Booth So by the end of the evening, would you say Sir David was drunk?
Sir David My lord, I must object. That is yet another outrageous leading question.
Blair-Booth All right, all right. We'll just leave it that Sir David came home smelling of alcohol and proceeded to drink two more bottles of wine. I doubt if even Sir David will be able to claim that is a leading question.
Sir David No, it's not even a question.
Blair-Booth (*to Mrs Rogers*) Now you were telling the court that you were looking for an excuse to return to the drawing-room?
Mrs Rogers Yes, I went in as soon as possible to give Lady Metcalfe her pills so she could have them and go to bed.
Blair-Booth And what were these pills, Mrs Rogers?
Mrs Rogers She takes a once-a-week pill once a week, and also a sleeping pill every night.
Blair-Booth What do you mean by a "once-a-week pill"?
Mrs Rogers It's a large red pill, it's very powerful and I'm afraid I cannot pronounce its name.
Blair-Booth My lord, I believe Mrs Rogers is referring to Cyclotoxelix. And on the night in question, did Lady Metcalfe take her once-a-week pill, the red one?
Mrs Rogers Yes.
Blair-Booth Then a white sleeping pill?
Mrs Rogers Yes, sir. At about a quarter to ten.
Blair-Booth So she should not have taken another red pill for at least seven days?

Mrs Rogers Correct, sir. Those were the clear instructions I was given by Dr
Weeden.

Blair-Booth I understand. And was Sir David in the room at the time?

Mrs Rogers Yes, he was.

Blair-Booth And did he witness what was going on?

Mrs Rogers Well, of course, he did. He was standing there, wasn't he?

Blair-Booth But could Sir David have had any way of knowing which pill
Lady Metcalfe was taking?

Mrs Rogers He must have known because when I give it to Lady Metcalfe I
always describe it as the "once-a-week" pill so he knew all right.

Blair-Booth Always? So Sir David had heard the expression before?

Mrs Rogers Many times.

Blair-Booth I see. And then what happened?

Mrs Rogers Lady Metcalfe and Sir David went up to the bedroom.

Blair-Booth And did you then go to bed?

Mrs Rogers Yes, but not until I had counted the red pills.

Blair-Booth And do you always do that?

Mrs Rogers Oh yes, always, sir.

Blair-Booth And how many red pills were there in the bottle?

Mrs Rogers There were seven.

Blair-Booth Seven? Are you certain, Mrs Rogers?

Mrs Rogers Yes, sir. I am certain.

Blair-Booth After you had gone to your own room, what happened next?

Mrs Rogers I fell asleep almost immediately, but was woken in the middle
of the night.

Blair-Booth At what time?

Mrs Rogers About three o'clock. I don't know what it was that woke me,
but I thought it must be Lady Metcalfe because she often wakes up in the
middle of the night and comes downstairs to make herself a cup of tea. So
I put on my dressing gown and went downstairs.

Blair-Booth And what did you see?

Mrs Rogers I saw Lady Metcalfe alone with Sir David.

Blair-Booth Yes?

Mrs Rogers I watched them from the stairs but they couldn't see me. He
was standing behind her. I saw him drop another once-a-week pill into
her tea. Poor Lady Metcalfe did not see what he had done, but I did.

Blair-Booth But Mrs Rogers, can you be certain which pill Sir David
dropped into her tea?

Mrs Rogers Oh yes, I saw it clearly.

Blair-Booth How can you be so sure?

Mrs Rogers Well, because of the colour. It was red. And anyway, I counted
them again later.

Blair-Booth You counted them again? How many were there this time?

Mrs Rogers Six.

Blair-Booth Six! When you saw Sir David had given the red pill to Lady
Metcalfe, why didn't you say something?

Mrs Rogers Because I feared what he might do to me.

Blair-Booth Feared what he might do to you? Please explain to the jury Mrs
Rogers, why you were frightened of him.

Mrs Rogers Because he has a very violent temper and because he often used to shout at me. Like he shouted at Lady Metcalfe. So I kept quiet as I was worried that if I said anything he might—well—hit me as well.

Blair-Booth I see. But subsequently you did make a statement to the police?

Mrs Rogers Yes, I felt it was wicked that he should be allowed to get away with it.

Blair-Booth You do understand the full consequences of what you are telling the court, Mrs Rogers?

Mrs Rogers Yes, I do. I watched him kill her.

Blair-Booth No more questions, my lord.

Mrs Rogers promptly starts to leave the witness box

Judge Just a moment, madam. I think Sir David may have some questions for you.

Sir David I certainly have, my lord. I would like to start, Mrs Rogers, with what you say you remember of the evening of twenty-third March.

Mrs Rogers I will remember everything that happened that night for the rest of my life. I will never forget it.

Sir David When you gave my wife her pills, where was I standing?

Mrs Rogers In the room with Lady Metcalfe.

Sir David Yes, but where in the room was I standing?

Mrs Rogers By the drinks table.

Sir David You're sure of that?

Mrs Rogers Yes. I am sure.

Sir David But that's at the other end of the room from where my wife was sitting—isn't it?

Mrs Rogers Yes.

Sir David So it's possible I couldn't have seen which pill Lady Metcalfe took?

Mrs Rogers (*a shrug*) I've no idea.

Sir David Exactly. Now, I should like to turn to what you say you saw a few hours later.

Mrs Rogers Wait a moment. I called it the once-a-week pill so you must have known.

Sir David We have only your word for that.

Mrs Rogers And we have only your word to say I didn't.

Sir David You say you stood on the stairs and saw me put a pill in my wife's tea?

Mrs Rogers Yes. I did.

Sir David And you knew that it was the Cyclotoxelix because the pill was red?

Mrs Rogers Yes.

Sir David All right. How far would you say it was from the stairs to the sofa, where Lady Metcalfe was sitting?

Mrs Rogers What do you mean?

Sir David I think you know exactly what I mean, but let me make it easier for you. Would you say you were at about the same distance from me then as you are now?

Mrs Rogers (*more confident now*) Yes. It's about the same distance.

Sir David Good. Then perhaps you can tell me the colour of the pills in these three bottles, Mrs Rogers. (*Sir David produces three full pill bottles from the shelf in the dock*)

Blair-Booth My lord, are we to be subjected to a conjuring trick by the defendant?

Judge I am as intrigued to find out as you are, Mr Blair-Booth—carry on, Sir David.

Sir David What colour are the pills in this bottle, Mrs Rogers?

Mrs Rogers Blue.

She is wrong. They are bright green. He holds up another bottle

Red.

She is right. He holds up another

Green.

She is wrong. The pills are blue

Sir David One out of three, Mrs Rogers. That could hardly be described as beyond reasonable doubt. And there were, if I am not mistaken, *two* bottles of pills by Lady Metcalfe's side. What was in the other bottle?

Mrs Rogers Her sleeping pills.

Blair-Booth whispers to Cole, his junior

Cole promptly leaves the court

Sir David And was Lady Metcalfe allowed to take more than one sleeping pill?

Mrs Rogers The doctor did not give me any instructions about them.

Sir David Then let me ask you, did Lady Metcalfe sometimes take more than one sleeping pill, if she could not get to sleep?

Mrs Rogers Yes. She did.

Sir David Then it might have been the sleeping pill, might it not, which you saw me put in my wife's tea?

Mrs Rogers No, it wasn't. It was the red once-a-week pill.

Sir David puts the pills back on the shelf under the dock rail

Sir David Is it possible that despite having worked for my wife for some considerable time you misunderstood the relationship between us?

Mrs Rogers What do you mean?

Sir David Exactly, what I say.

Judge (*intervening*) Mrs Rogers, do you think Sir David and Lady Metcalfe might have got on well together, but you didn't fully appreciate their relationship?

Mrs Rogers No, my lord, that is not possible. I watched them together over many years. Lady Metcalfe was a very charming woman, but Sir David was always drunk and shouting at both of us.

Sir David I think what Mrs Rogers is trying to tell the court, my lord, is that she doesn't like me.

Mrs Rogers No, I don't.

Sir David No, in fact, you don't have a good word to say for me—do you?

Mrs Rogers If there was anything good to say I would be happy to tell the Judge.

Sir David So you're only interested in saying harmful things.

Mrs Rogers No. I didn't say that. You're trying to put words into my mouth like you do with everybody. I only want the truth to come out.

Sir David The truth as you imagine you saw it—what was it you reported me as saying to my wife? "Woman, you will regret this"? Or words to that effect?

Mrs Rogers Yes.

Sir David And that I hit her.

Mrs Rogers Yes.

Sir David And then she begged for mercy?

Mrs Rogers Yes. I could hear it all clearly from the kitchen.

Sir David Have you ever heard of play-acting, Mrs Rogers? Is it not possible that you gained a totally false impression of what was really happening in the drawing-room?

Mrs Rogers I don't understand.

Sir David Agreed.

Since Sir David's attack was for the benefit of the jury, he doesn't mind. But the Judge intervenes

Judge I think you might have confused her, Sir David. I am not convinced myself that she fully understands.

Sir David I doubt she understands very much at all, my lord, except her own prejudices.

Cole enters with a bottle of white pills which he gives to Blair-Booth

Judge Sir David, that comment should not have been made. The jury will ignore it. Do you wish to re-examine this witness, Mr Blair-Booth?

Blair-Booth I do, my lord. Mrs Rogers ... about the test Sir David surprised you with ... you failed to distinguish between the green and the blue pills ... tell me—did Lady Metcalfe have any blue or green pills?

Mrs Rogers No ... only red ... and white.

Blair-Booth Exactly. And the colour you did identify correctly was red. (*He suddenly holds up a bottle of white pills*) Can you tell me, Mrs Rogers, the colour of the pills in this bottle?

Mrs Rogers hesitates only slightly

Mrs Rogers White.

Blair-Booth Correct. Thank you. No more questions, my lord.

The Judge indicates that Mrs Rogers can stand down

I would like to call Dr John Weeden.

Dr Weeden enters

The Usher administers the full oath

Blair-Booth Are you Dr John Weeden, of thirteen Beckers Hill Drive, Wimbledon?

Weeden I am.

Blair-Booth Are you a registered medical practitioner?

Weeden Yes.

Blair-Booth And were you the late Lady Millicent Metcalfe's doctor?

Weeden Yes ... and Sir David's.

Blair-Booth Dr Weeden, would you please tell the court how you came to hear of Lady Metcalfe's death.

Weeden Sir David called me in the early hours of March twenty-fourth. I went to his house immediately but, when I arrived Lady Metcalfe was already dead.

Blair-Booth At what time was that, Dr Weeden?

Weeden Sir David called me around half-past five in the morning. I must have reached his home a little after six.

Blair-Booth And what hour would you have put the time of death?

Weeden Approximately four a.m.

Blair-Booth Four a.m.

Weeden Yes.

Blair-Booth So, when Sir David called you, his wife must have been dead for some time.

Weeden I assume so.

Blair-Booth Did it in any way concern you, Doctor, that Sir David had waited for over an hour before he got in touch with you.

Weeden No. It's not uncommon for a bereaved husband or wife to remain a considerable time alone with their dead spouse before letting anyone know. Sometimes they refuse to accept death has actually taken place.

Blair-Booth And in your professional opinion this was death by natural causes?

Weeden Yes.

Blair-Booth Would you describe yourself as a close friend of Sir David Metcalfe, Dr Weeden.

Weeden I would like to think so.

Sir David (*interjecting*) What is the purpose of this line of questioning, my lord? Is Mr Blair-Booth suggesting a conspiracy?

Judge I hope that is not the case, Mr Blair-Booth?

Blair-Booth Far from it, my lord, Sir David wrongs me. It is, in fact, the exact opposite I am trying to establish, namely that Dr Weeden was purposely misled into believing that this was a death by natural causes. Whereas in fact Sir David knew exactly what he had done. So, Dr Weeden, at no time did you suspect that Lady Metcalfe had been given an overdose of drugs?

Weeden (*firmly*) At no time.

Blair-Booth Would you describe Lady Metcalfe as the kind of person who might take her own life?

Weeden No, sir. Though one can never be sure in these cases.

Blair-Booth Dr Weeden, did you write out the prescription for Cyclotoxelix?

Weeden Yes, I did.

Blair-Booth When?

Weeden (*checking his notes*) On February twenty-third.

Blair-Booth How many pills did you prescribe?
Weeden Twelve.
Blair-Booth Twelve?
Weeden Yes. Enough to last three months.
Blair-Booth At one a week?
Weeden Yes.
Blair-Booth So ... (*He refers to his pocket diary*) February twenty-third—
they started immediately?
Weeden Yes.
Blair-Booth March second ... ninth ... sixteenth ... twenty-third. Five
weeks?
Weeden Yes.
Blair-Booth And there should have been how many remaining?

As Weeden hesitates

Seven?
Weeden Yes, I suppose so.
Blair-Booth You suppose so? Have I miscounted?
Weeden No.
Blair-Booth No. But you didn't actually count how many pills were left?
Weeden I did, but not in the sense you mean. It was just to check how many
there were.
Blair-Booth I see. And even that did not make you revise your opinion as to
the cause of death?
Weeden No.
Blair-Booth Well, perhaps I can. Tell me, Doctor, could anyone who had
read the label on the bottle be left in any doubt as to what the result of an
overdose might be?
Weeden I don't think so.
Blair-Booth Let's be absolutely sure, shall we, Dr Weeden? Will you be so
kind as to read out to the Court the instructions as they are printed on the
label. (*Blair-Booth addresses the Judge*) My lord, Exhibit One.

The Usher takes the bottle to Weeden

Yes, Dr Weeden?
Weeden "Cyclotoxelix. One pill two and a half grams, every seven days.
Keep in a locked cupboard. Any excess of the prescribed drug could prove
fatal."
Blair-Booth (*emphasizing the words*) Could—prove—fatal. Admirably
clear, Doctor. Yet you were surprised by the police investigation and the
pathologist's report?
Weeden Yes, I was.
Blair-Booth And, one final point, Dr Weeden. When you examined Lady
Metcalfe, did you find any bruises on her?
Weeden Yes, I found an extensive bruise on the outside of her right forearm
which——
Blair-Booth (*interrupting*) Could that have been caused by a blow?
Weeden Well, I suppose it could, but——

Blair-Booth From a bottle, perhaps?

Weeden Unlikely, I would have thought.

Blair-Booth Why? If I aimed a blow at you with a bottle ... (*he mimes*) ... and you warded that blow off with your arm ... ? (*He mimes again*)

Weeden Well, it's possible but——

Blair-Booth It's possible.

Weeden (*reluctantly*) Yes——

Blair-Booth Thank you, Doctor. Wait there. (*He sits*)

Sir David Dr Weeden, how long have you been Lady Metcalfe's doctor?

Weeden Seventeen years.

Sir David So it would be fair to say you knew the family well?

Weeden Yes, I had that privilege.

Sir David At the time in question, was Lady Metcalfe suffering from any illness?

Weeden Yes. I had been treating her for the previous fourteen months for Lymphosarcoma.

Sir David What, Dr Weeden, is that in layman's language?

Weeden Cancer of the lymph glands.

Sir David And was Lady Metcalfe on drugs?

Weeden Yes. Cyclotoxelix.

Sir David And she was in considerable pain?

Weeden Frequently. One might almost say, constantly. It was only her tremendous courage that gave her the will to live.

Sir David Then her death might have been a blessing in disguise?

Blair-Booth Objection, my lord. Dr Weeden cannot be asked to pronounce on the innermost thoughts of the Almighty.

Judge I agree. Members of the jury, you will ignore that last statement. Tread more carefully, Sir David.

Sir David I apologize, my lord.

Judge You need not answer the last question, Dr Weeden.

Weeden *I* prayed that she would die.

Judge I beg your pardon, Dr Weeden.

Weeden I prayed that she would die, my lord. She was such a good person. She did not deserve to be in such pain.

Judge (*sternly*) The jury must disregard that statement as well. It has no bearing on this case. Please pursue a new line of questioning, Sir David.

Sir David As you wish, my lord. I'd like to return to the bruise on my wife's arm, Dr Weeden, which my learned friend emphasized in his earlier examination. Did I give you a full explanation as to how that bruise came about?

Weeden Yes, you did. You informed me that Lady Metcalfe had stumbled and fallen.

Sir David Was the bruise consistent with such a fall?

Weeden Yes. One automatically throws out an arm to break such a fall ...

Sir David I see. Dr Weeden, you have testified that Lady Metcalfe was in considerable pain from an incurable cancer, for which you had been administering drugs to her for the past fourteen months?

Weeden Yes.

Sir David Would you say, Doctor, that she was on the point of death and might even have died that night?
Weeden It's possible.
Sir David And would it have ever crossed your mind that I could have murdered my wife with an overdose of drugs?
Weeden Never.
Sir David Could there be any other explanation of this overdosage?
Weeden In my view, yes. Lady Metcalfe had been on these drugs for a considerable period of time, which would have produced a general build-up——

Blair-Booth is on his feet

Blair-Booth My lord, the pathologist's report——
Judge I agree, Mr Blair-Booth. (*To Weeden*) Dr Weeden, I fully understand how unpleasant it is for you to give evidence in a trial involving a close friend, but it does not give you the liberty to offer personal opinions that contradict agreed evidence. The jury must once again disregard that statement.
Sir David Returning to the Cyclotoxelix pills. There were only six left in the bottle . . .
Weeden Yes.
Sir David And there should have been seven?

As Weeden nods . . .

So an excessive amount had been taken?
Weeden Apparently, yes.
Sir David But not necessarily on that particular evening.
Blair-Booth (*rising*) My lord . . .
Judge Yes, Mr Blair-Booth. (*To the "jury"*) Members of the jury. The pathologist's report clearly indicated that a considerable excess of recently taken Cyclotoxelix was found in the body, an amount inconsistent with the suggestion of Sir David and Dr Weeden. (*To Sir David*) Do you intend to pursue this?
Sir David No, my lord, I have no further questions. Thank you, Dr Weeden.
Judge Do you wish to re-examine, Mr Blair-Booth?
Blair-Booth I certainly do, my lord. Dr Weeden, you say that Lady Metcalfe was near death and it is possible that she might have died that night. I must ask you, was it possible or probable?
Weeden Possible.
Blair-Booth *Not* probable. And if she had not died that night of an overdose of Cyclotoxelix as was clearly stated in the pathologist's report, how long do you think she might have hoped to live, at the outside?
Weeden Oh, I couldn't venture an opinion on that.
Blair-Booth Come, now, Dr Weeden, there's no need to be coy. You told the court that it was your professional opinion she *might* have died that night. You can surely let us know how long she *might* have hoped to live?
Weeden Well, I suppose she *might* have lived another two, possibly three years.

Blair-Booth *Three years?*
Weeden It's possible—at the outside.
Blair-Booth Is it? Then I should like to ask your professional opinion on something else. (*He glances through his notes*) Lymphosarcoma ... is research being done on this kind of cancer, with a hope for a breakthrough that might save cases like Lady Metcalfe?
Weeden Extensive research is being carried out, at the Chester Beattie Institute in particular, but to date there's been no sign of a breakthrough.
Blair-Booth Well, let me ask you, do you think a breakthrough *is* possible in the next three years ...
Weeden (*immediately regretting having spoken too quickly*) Well, it must be *possible* ... yes.
Blair-Booth "It must be possible, yes." Thank you, Dr Weeden. No more questions, my lord. I call Lionel Hamilton.

Lionel Hamilton enters the witness box and bows to the Judge

The Usher administers the full oath

You are Lionel Hamilton, a solicitor of the Supreme Court and a senior partner of Hamilton, Gray and Co.
Hamilton Yes, sir.
Blair-Booth And your firm were the solicitors to the late Lady Metcalfe and to Sir David Metcalfe?
Hamilton We have that honour.
Blair-Booth Did Lady Metcalfe leave a will, Mr Hamilton?
Hamilton She did, sir.
Blair-Booth And who were the beneficiaries?
Hamilton A few charities received small amounts but the bulk of the estate was left to her husband, Sir David Metcalfe.
Blair-Booth Mm, hm. What is the extent of the, er, *bulk* of the estate, Mr Hamilton?
Sir David (*rising*) Is this relevant, my lord?
Judge I suspect we're about to find out, Sir David. Please continue, Mr Hamilton.
Hamilton The home in Wimbledon in which they lived.
Blair-Booth And who owned that house, Mr Hamilton?
Hamilton Lady Metcalfe.
Blair-Booth And what else did Lady Metcalfe leave her husband?
Hamilton Some shares and cash.
Blair-Booth I see. So the total value of Sir David's inheritance was ... ?

As Hamilton hesitates ...

There must have been a value placed on the estate, Mr Hamilton, for probate. If we deduct the gifts to charities, what would that figure be ... ?
Hamilton Including the house?
Blair-Booth Yes, the full value of Sir David's inheritance.
Hamilton (*hesitating again*) Just over one million pounds.
Blair-Booth Just over one million pounds.
Hamilton Less than a third of that would be in cash, of course.

Blair-Booth Yes, of course ... well ... so for the first time in his life, Sir David found himself a rich man?

Hamilton I would say, with respect, sir, that for the first time in his life, he found himself a poor man.

Blair-Booth Is he not now extremely wealthy?

Hamilton That depends on how you measure wealth, Mr Blair-Booth.

Blair-Booth Well, I agree with you, Mr Hamilton. Had I over a million pounds, I would consider myself extremely wealthy. As, I've no doubt, would most members of the jury, if not all of them put together. I have no further questions, my lord.

Sir David Mr Hamilton, there is no suggestion, is there, that I was at any time financially embarrassed?

Hamilton Not to my knowledge, Sir David.

Sir David Or that I was in any particular need of money?

Hamilton No, sir. You have received for many years a most healthy income from the Bar, where your services were greatly sought after.

Sir David How long have you known my wife and myself?

Hamilton I have served you both for over twenty years.

Sir David And what was your opinion of our relationship?

Hamilton Above reproach. One could only admire, indeed envy, you both.

Blair-Booth (*aside to Cole*) "O good and faithful servant".

Sir David Thank you, Mr Hamilton. No more questions, my lord.

Blair-Booth Can I ask you, Mr Hamilton, how often you saw Lady Metcalfe and Sir David together?

As Hamilton hesitates ...

Once a day, once a week, once a month ... ?

Hamilton I couldn't give an exact——

Blair-Booth (*cutting in*) Perhaps once a year?

Hamilton No, no. Nearer to once a month.

Blair-Booth Then isn't it possible that Sir David, when in your presence, was able to put on an act of caring for Lady Metcalfe, and that only someone living in the same house, watching them every day, might observe the truth?

Hamilton If that was the case, sir, it was an act sustained over a period of twenty years without one bad performance from either party.

Blair-Booth That would depend on how you imagined you saw it. No more questions, my lord. That concludes the case for the Crown, my lord. I shall be calling no more witnesses.

Judge Very well. Then I think we might rise for lunch. We'll resume again at two o'clock.

Usher Be upstanding in court.

Black-out

The Lights come up again

As they do so, the Judge is entering. He bows and is bowed to by all in the Court

Cole is outside the courtroom. Hamilton is now sitting directly next to Pierson. Sir David crosses from the dock to the witness box during the next few lines

Judge Mr Pierson ... will you be calling any witnesses?
Pierson Only Sir David Metcalfe, my lord.
Judge As you wish.

Cole rushes in and goes quickly to Blair-Booth with a paper

Cole I've just been handed this by our instructing solicitor.
Blair-Booth Follow it up immediately. Get me the exact figures. But don't put it in front of me unless it will stand up. I'll keep him on his feet as long as I can.

Cole exits

Sir David I swear by Almighty God that the evidence I shall give shall be the truth, the whole truth, and nothing but the truth.

Pierson looks towards the box to question him

Pierson You are Sir David Metcalfe, one of Her Majesty's Counsel, learned in the law, and you reside at forty-four, The Oaks, Wimbledon?
Sir David Yes.
Pierson Can you tell the jury in your own words, Sir David, what happened on the evening of the twenty-third March, this year, and the early morning of the twenty-fourth ...?
Sir David Yes. After being held up in court, I decided to have a quick dinner at my club and arrived home a little after eight-thirty. My wife seemed depressed so I opened a bottle of wine in the hope it would cheer her up. It—or I—raised her spirits for a while, but I suspect she must have, once again, been concealing considerable pain. Some time before ten, after she had taken her pills, I helped her up to bed.
Pierson And then what happened, Sir David?
Sir David I, too, went to bed and fell asleep quickly. But at about three o'clock, I was woken by a noise which seemed to come from downstairs. Alarmed when I discovered my wife was not at my side, I ran downstairs, where I found Millicent lying on the drawing-room floor. I picked her up and helped her to the sofa.
Pierson Was she unconscious?
Sir David No, but badly shaken by her fall.
Pierson Then what happened, Sir David?
Sir David She asked if I could make her a cup of tea. I went to the kitchen immediately. When I returned, with the tea, the pain was obviously much worse than it had been the previous evening. She had the pill bottles in her hands. She was fumbling with one of them, trying to open it. She handed them to me and asked if I would put one of the pills in her tea, which I did.
Pierson What colour was the pill she handed you?
Sir David I can't remember. I was at the time only concerned with my wife's condition. I prayed she would find relief in the medicine ...
Pierson Yes?
Sir David And then, thank God, she did. I took the tea away from her and she seemed to slip into a restful sleep. I considered it better to just hold on to her, rather than to try and get her back to bed, perhaps disturbing her. And then ... she started to grow cold ... and I could no longer hear her

breathing. I tried to find a pulse, but could feel nothing. (*He pauses*) That was when I called Dr Weeden. He came right away ... within the hour ... and confirmed my worst fears.

Pierson I see. I apologize for the next question, Sir David, aware of all you've been through. Were you happily married, or is it as your housekeeper suggests, that you quarrelled continually during the evening in question?

Sir David We did not quarrel, Mr Pierson. The only things we ever disagreed about were Dylan Thomas and cricket. I only wish she were still alive so that I could quarrel with her now.

Pierson Thank you, Sir David. No more questions, my lord.

Judge Mr Blair-Booth?

Blair-Booth Sir David, have you conducted many murder defences over the years?

Sir David Many.

Blair-Booth And have you had a high success rate?

Sir David One that you would be pleased with no doubt.

Blair-Booth And does this experience stretch to murder by poisoning?

Sir David (*hesitating*) It does.

Blair-Booth So this is not a new experience for you?

Sir David Not exactly but ...

Blair-Booth So you would know only too well how to present a good defence in a weak case, wouldn't you Sir David?

Sir David Yes, but——

Blair-Booth (*cutting in brutally*) I don't have to remind you of all people, Sir David, only to answer the questions put to you—so let us at least agree on one thing. You have no rival at the Bar when it comes to defending a weak case. The jury can rest assured they are up against the expert.

Sir David You were never willing to admit as much in the past.

Blair-Booth Tell me first, do you believe Mrs Rogers, your housekeeper, to be a dishonest person?

Sir David No, but——

Blair-Booth So, in your opinion, Mrs Rogers is an honest soul, so let us return to *her* account of the night of the twenty-third March. Did you, earlier in that evening, strike your wife after she had accused you of drunkenness?

Sir David Certainly not, we were only play-acting, not at all serious and I only pretended to hit her.

Blair-Booth Play-acting, not serious? You only pretended to hit her? Yet that pretence caused very real, actual bruising on her forearm?

Sir David The bruising was caused by my wife falling while I was in the bedroom.

Blair-Booth We only have your word for that, Sir David. Now you amused us all a moment ago by telling us that you only ever quarrelled with your wife over Dylan Thomas or cricket ... but is that entirely accurate? Didn't you have a more serious quarrel that evening having arrived home late—and drunk?

Sir David I was not late, in the sense of being beyond any appointed hour. I had been delayed in court, and then had something to eat, at my club.

Blair-Booth And drink, Sir David.

Sir David Yes, I had a little wine.

Blair-Booth If your wife was in so much pain, might it not have been more considerate for you to have gone straight home to be with her as any loving husband would in such circumstances?

Sir David I always tried to put her to as little inconvenience as possible.

Blair-Booth By coming home drunk and starting a quarrel.

Sir David We did not quarrel.

Blair-Booth Not even a "mock quarrel"?

Sir David A mock quarrel, perhaps.

Blair-Booth Overheard by Mrs Rogers?

Sir David So she claims.

Blair-Booth Mock threatening to hit your wife?

Sir David Play-acting, joking.

Blair-Booth Play-acting? Joking? With a dying wife?

Sir David Oh, for heaven's sake. I was trying to keep her spirits up.

Blair-Booth By shouting at her?

Sir David Yes. Married couples over the years develop their own private brand of humour. It is not meant to be shared by the public or dissected in court.

Blair-Booth This was certainly not meant to be shared by the public or dissected in court, for had it been, they too, might have misunderstood.

Sir David Yes.

Blair-Booth As Mrs Rogers misunderstood.

Sir David Yes.

Blair-Booth And as others might also misunderstand. Yes. Well let's turn to something else, Sir David. Had you drunk a lot before you arrived home that night?

Sir David No more than usual.

Blair-Booth That is a singularly uninformative answer, Sir David. But I won't embarrass you by asking you to quantify what is "usual". Let us just turn to what you had to drink *after* your usual. (*He refers to his notes*) Two bottles of Mouton Rothschild ... nineteen sixty-one ... before you retired to bed?

Sir David Yes.

Blair-Booth And you wouldn't describe that as excessive?

Sir David Not in the circumstances.

Blair-Booth Circumstances?

Sir David I was depressed—we both were—about my wife's continuing illness.

Blair-Booth You don't think it was your excessive drinking that caused your wife such distress?

Sir David No. I am not an alcoholic, Mr Blair-Booth, if that's what you're driving at.

Blair-Booth Alcoholic, did I mention the word?

Sir David No, sir, but it's what you meant.

Blair-Booth That is not what I meant, sir. But it was your excessive drinking that made you quarrel with your wife. That is what I meant.

Sir David (*shouting*) We did not quarrel at all that night. Mrs Rogers has entirely misunderstood the relationship between my wife and myself.

Blair-Booth (*quietly*) If you raise your voice any louder, Sir David, it is possible that the jury might also misunderstand, and think that you did lose your temper that night. So let us sum up then, you did not quarrel because you were late, or because you had drunk too much, and you did not hit your wife ... Mrs Rogers imagined all these things which can, in fact, be explained away by a picture of normal wedded bliss.

Sir David If you had ever married, Mr Blair-Booth, you might begin to understand.

Blair-Booth Let us now turn to the estate of the late Lady Metcalfe, and the beneficiary. Do I understand that because of your wife's death you have come into a fortune of just over one million pounds ... ?

Sir David Including the house, yes.

Blair-Booth What was your personal financial position while Lady Metcalfe was still alive?

Sir David I had a few shares and a small overdraft.

Blair-Booth That sounds very modest, Sir David. You must spend a good deal. How much does a bottle of Mouton Rothschild cost? The sixty-one vintage?

Sir David I'm sure you've already enquired, Mr Blair-Booth, but I wouldn't know. I was fortunate enough to inherit my wine-cellar.

Blair-Booth Another inheritance? You weren't married before, Sir David?

Sir David No. It came from my former Head of Chambers.

Blair-Booth Who obviously knew your habits.

Sir David Who also knew that I prefer fine wine to inferior cross-examination.

Cole enters and goes straight to Blair-Booth

Blair-Booth Would your lordship grant me a moment?

Judge Certainly.

Blair-Booth then studies the file Cole has handed him

Blair-Booth Sir David, I'd like to return to your financial position.

Pierson My lord, I must object. Is this leading anywhere?

Judge I think it's time you came to the point, Mr Blair-Booth. If there is one.

Blair-Booth Oh, there is indeed, my lord. Sir David, can you confirm that immediately preceeding your wife's death, you owed the city stock-brokers, Gilbert and Goddard, two hundred and eighty-one thousand pounds? And that you were being pressed for payment?

Sir David Yes. I had invested in some shares on the advice of an old friend. The shares plummeted when the rumour of a takeover bid failed to materialize. Unfortunately, I found myself unable to pay the full amount when the account became due.

Blair-Booth "Rumour of a takeover bid", "on the advice of an old friend". Wouldn't it be accurate to say that Government Inspectors were sent in to go over the company books because they suspected "insider trading"?

Sir David Yes, sir, but I knew nothing of it.

Blair-Booth So *you* were not involved in the "insider trading"?

Sir David If I had been I wouldn't have lost all my money.

Blair-Booth "All your money", Sir David. Did I hear you correctly? *All* your money. Now that we have established that, let us try to discover how this came about. You bought shares without actually having the money to pay for them?

Sir David On margin, yes. It is an established city practice.

Blair-Booth Something you've done before?

Sir David Once or twice.

Blair-Booth Then would I be right in saying that this was not your first share transaction to have ended so disastrously.

Sir David I've had a run of rather bad luck, lately, yes.

Blair-Booth So, shares had been purchased in your name with money you did not have, and now you were being pressed to pay. Two hundred and eighty-one thousand pounds?

Sir David Yes, I was.

Blair-Booth In the period immediately preceeding your wife's death?

Sir David Yes.

Blair-Booth And by whom were you being pressed? Gilbert and Goddard?

Sir David Yes. A Mr Holbrook. A junior partner.

Blair-Booth So it was Mr Holbrook who was pressing you in particular?

Sir David Yes.

Blair-Booth In what way?

Sir David At the time, by impertinent phone calls. He was worried that if I did not pay in time, he would lose his job.

Blair-Booth I'm not surprised. And did he phone you at home?

Sir David Yes, and even at my chambers.

Blair-Booth Oh dear, how very inconvenient. What would have happened if you had failed to pay the debt in time? I mean, to your career, Sir David?

Sir David You know the answer to that, Mr Blair-Booth. I would undoubtedly have been disbarred as a practising barrister.

Blair-Booth And no doubt had to resign as Chairman of the Bar Council?

Sir David Yes.

Blair-Booth How very embarrassing. But happily, you have been able to repay your debt with the money so conveniently left to you by your late wife?

Sir David Yes, I have.

Blair-Booth Finally then, Sir David . . . on the fatal evening in question . . . did you see your wife take her pills before she retired to bed?

Sir David Yes, but I was on the other side of the room.

Blair-Booth But did you see her take a pill from both bottles?

Sir David I believe she did, yes.

Blair-Booth And did you hear Mrs Rogers say that she must take her "once-a-week" pill?

Sir David Yes, I believe I made some joke about it.

Blair-Booth Another joke? Did your wife laugh this time? Not long after your wife had retired, you too went to bed?

Sir David Yes.

Blair-Booth And then you claim that what woke you was the noise of your wife falling?

Sir David Yes, although I didn't realize at the time what it was.

Blair-Booth You then ran downstairs, made her a cup of tea, and she passed *you* the bottle of pills?

Sir David That is exactly what happened.

Blair-Booth What was the colour of the pill you administered?

Sir David I really can't remember.

Blair-Booth You can't remember. The pill was in your hand. You saw it. You put it in the tea and you can't remember? Why didn't you study the label on the bottle before administering the pill?

Sir David I *assumed* that as Millie had handed me the bottle, she knew what she was doing.

Blair-Booth You *assumed*, Sir David. You *claim* that Lady Metcalfe was in extreme pain, and deeply depressed. You *claim* that she had fallen heavily, thus bruising herself. But you still *assumed* that she knew what she was doing when she handed you a bottle of pills which were to be taken only once a week. Surely a husband as *devoted* as yourself would have at least checked the label. Unless of course you wanted to give your wife two once-a-week pills within a few hours. I suggest, Sir David, you knew very well what *you* were doing. Here was an easy way out, a chance to clear yourself of embarrassing debts, an ailing wife, and the collapse of your career. I suggest, Sir David, had the whole episode not been witnessed by your housekeeper, the honest and courageous Mrs Rogers, the truth would still lie buried at the bottom of a grave in Wimbledon. The truth is, Sir David, you assumed too much. You *assumed* you had committed the perfect murder.

Sir David No, sir. That is not what happened.

Blair-Booth Do you deny having drunk too much that night?

Sir David No.

Blair-Booth Do you deny that you were embarrassed by a substantial debt you could not meet?

Sir David No.

Blair-Booth Do you deny that your wife's death allowed you to clear that debt?

Sir David No.

Blair-Booth Do you deny that you administered the fatal pill?

Sir David No, I cannot.

Blair-Booth Then can you deny that you wilfully murdered your wife?

Sir David I can and I do.

Blair-Booth No more questions, my lord.

Judge Do you wish to re-examine Sir David, Mr Pierson?

Pierson Yes, my lord. Just a few questions. If Lady Metcalfe had known of this debt, how would you have expected her to react?

Blair-Booth Objection, my lord. How could anyone possibly know how Lady Metcalfe might have reacted?

Judge Sir David might, he was, after all, her husband. But the question is somewhat hypothetical, Mr Pierson.

Pierson Yes, my lord. Sir David, *had* you mentioned the debt to Lady Metcalfe?

Sir David No. I had intended to do so ... but the right occasion never presented itself.

Pierson So your motive in *not* telling her was ...?

Sir David At all times, a consideration for her peace of mind. The debt did not bother me personally: I would have repaid it in due course.

Pierson How?

Sir David From substantial fees due to me, and still outstanding.

Pierson Sir David, I put to you the same questions as the prosecution, but without malice. Did you have too much to drink that night?

Sir David In the sense that it affected my judgement, no.

Pierson Could your financial embarrassment have motivated you to murder?

Sir David Of Holbrook, perhaps ... for his impertinent telephone calls. Of my wife—never.

Pierson Did you love your wife?

Sir David Deeply. She brought wit and humour, gentleness and understanding into my life, and made our marriage an experience of happiness I shall never forget, or cease to be grateful for. Yes, sir. I loved her.

Pierson Did you murder Lady Metcalfe?

Sir David I did not. I assure you, I did not.

Pierson Thank you, Sir David. I shall be calling no more witnesses, my lord. That concludes the case for the defence.

Judge Thank you, Mr Pierson.

Sir David crosses from the witness box to the dock. As he does so, the Lights fade to a spot on the Judge

Members of the jury, let me conclude my summing up by saying that it is not my duty to guide you in any particular direction, or to let you know my opinion. I am called the Judge but you are the judges. I can only direct you on the law and the law is straightforward. The burden of proof is on the prosecution. They must make certain of guilt beyond reasonable doubt. A man is guilty of murder if, without lawful excuse, he causes, with intent, the death of another. That is the law, and you are the sole judges of act in this case. When you have weighed all the evidence as it has been presented to you, you will have to decide upon your verdict. It would be quite wrong for me to give you any idea as to what I think. The verdict is yours alone. Put out of your mind, anger, sympathy and all other emotions. If the evidence does not satisfy you beyond reasonable doubt you will bring a verdict of "Not Guilty", but on the other hand, if it does, your verdict, however unpalatable it may be—must be "Guilty". I do not envy you your task but you must be resolute in your duty. When the Jury

Bailiff has been sworn, you will retire to consider your verdict and in due course return and let me know how you find.

The Lights come up again. The Usher stands up

Usher I swear by Almighty God that I will well and truly keep this jury in some convenient and private place with such accommodation as the court shall direct. I will not suffer any person to speak to them, neither will I speak to them myself touching the trial had here this day without leave of the court unless it be to ask them if they have agreed on their verdict.

The Lights fade to spots on the Clerk and Sir David

Clerk Will the defendant please rise.

The Lights come up to full

Will the foreman of the jury please stand. Mr Foreman, do you find the prisoner, Sir David Metcalfe, guilty or not guilty of murder?

Everyone onstage stares fixedly at the audience

Black-out

CURTAIN

The front door slams, off

Goodness. Almost on time for a change. (*She composes herself, smiles welcomingly as ...*)

Sir David bursts into the room—it's the only way he knows how to enter. In his early fifties, of distinguished appearance, he exudes endless energy. He wears a dark overcoat with a velvet collar and carries a battered, swollen briefcase. He drops the briefcase with a thud and takes off his coat, handing it to Mrs Rogers as though she were a mobile clothes-rack

Mrs Rogers takes Sir David's coat off to the hall then crosses back and exits right to the kitchen

Sir David Sorry I'm a bit late, darling ... I made the mistake of dropping in at the club, and then couldn't escape Benson ... "A word in your ear, dear boy". Are you all right, darling? Have you had a good day?

Lady Metcalfe Not bad, David, but I can't pretend I've done a lot. (*She gives him a little hug, then breaks away*) I thought about pruning the rose bed, but in the end, I only thought about it.

Sir David Good, because you are supposed to be taking things easy.

Lady Metcalfe I am, all I did today was to decant the wine, then I just collapsed on the sofa and let Mrs Rogers get on with preparing the dinner. She really is a gem.

Sir David A gem is not how I would describe her.

Lady Metcalfe (*smiling*) Nor she you.

Sir David Shall I get you a drink?

Lady Metcalfe There isn't time, David—you really must go and change.

Sir David I will, I will. Don't fuss. I'm the original quick-change artist. I should have been in vaudeville.

Lady Metcalfe I thought you were in vaudeville.

Sir David Millie ...

Lady Metcalfe David, do hurry, you know very well when that clock strikes eight, Mr Hamilton will be standing on the doorstep.

Sir David Damn it ... yes ... has the man never been late?

Lady Metcalfe Not once in the twenty years I've known him.

Sir David exits

...ause. The carriage clock strikes eight; on the third chime, the doorbell rings

...rs Rogers enters, crosses to the front door off left, then enters left, ...llowed by Lionel Hamilton

...Rogers Sir Lionel Hamilton.

...Rogers exits

...etcalfe *Mister* Hamilton. I'm sorry, Lionel. Mrs Rogers thinks ...ne who comes here must have a title. She's a frightful snob.

...Don't let it worry you, dear lady.

...alfe Now, what would you like to drink?

...hall I help myself?

...fe Please do—David should join us soon. He's just changing.

ACT II

Before the trial

Scene 1

*The drawing-room of the Wimbledon home of Sir David and Lady Metcalfe.
The dining-room is adjacent. Its double doors are closed. It is an early evening
in Spring, about nine months before the trial*

*Lady Metcalfe, in her late forties, beautiful and elegantly dressed for a dinner
party, is speaking on the telephone*

Lady Metcalfe Yes, my dear ... the trial begins tomorrow. ... Why is
David defending her? I really don't know. He just can't resist impossible
cases, can he? (*She listens, occasionally glancing at her wrist-watch*) That's
right ... yes, murdered her lover ... stabbed him seven times ... yes ...
Rusty scissors? Well, I don't suppose the rust is that relevant ... (*She
listens*) But only *her* fingerprints—precisely. I imagine that's the problem.
... Oh, tonight? We're having one of our usual pre-trial dinners. It gives
David a chance to rehearse those brilliant off-the-cuff remarks he's so
famous for.

Mrs Rogers enters from the hall

(*To Mrs Rogers*) Mrs Rogers, could you bring the wine and glass
please?

Mrs Rogers exits to the dining-room leaving the doors open

(*On the phone*) Exactly ... Lionel Hamilton's coming, the ~~~
of —— Yes, that's right. And Robert Pierson, David's ~
you've met him ...

*Mrs Rogers enters with the wine, leaving the upstag~
doors open*

Dark-haired and sexy? (*She thinks*) I suppose he
I'll tell David you called. ... Your paper cal~
Scissor Stabber? Good heavens! *The Tim~*
accused. All right, I must rush now, l~
Goodbye. (*She puts the phone down fir~
her thoughts*) Now, Mrs Rogers ... ~

Mrs Rogers They are, my lady.

Lady Metcalfe Good. Then if you'~
my husband isn't too appallin~

Hamilton A little whisky and a lot of water. Can I get you something?
Lady Metcalfe No, I'm fine, thank you.
Hamilton I do so enjoy these dinner parties, not to mention the company.
Lady Metcalfe I wonder David doesn't invite the judge.
Hamilton Now then, what have you got up your sleeve for us tonight? Do you remember your menu for Humphries, the Ascot arson killer?
Lady Metcalfe Smoked ham and steak *flambé.*
Hamilton Charles McCulloch, the body in the freezer? Vichysoisse, a cold collation . . .
Lady Metcalfe And baked Alaska.
Hamilton Lang, the hatchet murderer . . . bortsch and spare ribs.
Lady Metcalfe How appropriate. What a good memory you have, Lionel. Perhaps I should write a cook book. Everyone else seems to be. I shall call it "Forty Forensic Feasts".
Hamilton You are a wonderful hostess, my dear.
Lady Metcalfe And you are an old flatterer. As if this was the only place you dine well.
Hamilton It is.
Lady Metcalfe Don't you gorge yourself regularly at the Law Society?
Hamilton My dear lady, the Law Society employs the same caterers as Paddington Station. Brown Windsor soup and shepherd's pie, but I must admit the salmonella is always fresh. The only other contract they haven't lost is for the House of Lords, whose nannies had already told them that good food was only for sissies. No, no. You're the last refuge of an old bachelor.

The sound of the front door-bell and of Mrs Rogers hurrying to open it

Lady Metcalfe Ah . . . that must be Robert.
Hamilton Pierson? Soon to be a QC, I'm told.
Lady Metcalfe I hadn't heard.
Hamilton Then please forget I mentioned it, dear lady.

Mrs Rogers enters with Pierson

Mrs Rogers Mr Pierson.

Mrs Rogers exits

Lady Metcalfe Robert.
Pierson Millie.
Lady Metcalfe Your usual?
Pierson Thank you. Good-evening, sir.
Hamilton Good-evening.
Pierson Where's the great man? Don't tell me he's not home yet?
Lady Metcalfe No, he managed to beat you by a few minutes, but you're quite right. He did look in at the Garrick Club *en route* and got held up, of course.
Hamilton Benson, no doubt?

Sir David enters

Sir David Benson, indeed. Do you know, I was once guest of honour at a dinner where the dear fellow was entrusted with the responsibility of introducing me. "I should now like to introduce you to Sir David Metcalfe, who is well known to you all for his debatable qualities. Sir David, as you all know, is one of our greatest advocates, and the secret of advocacy is honesty. Once you can fake that, the rest is easy."

He continues to the drinks table, to help himself. The others laugh

Lady Metcalfe David, while I think of it, your mother rang.
Sir David What did she want?
Lady Metcalfe Oh, just to run over your defence for the "Sevenoaks Scissor Stabber" . . .
Sir David The "Sevenoaks Scissor Stabber"? She must still be reading the *Daily Express*. (*To Robert*) Mouton Rothschild sixty-one, left to me by the late Head of Chambers, Danvers Gray, who tried manfully to finish it all before he departed this world. Had he managed the three score years and ten which he considered no more than the legal contract with his maker—he would undoubtedly have polished off the lot.
Lady Metcalfe With your assistance, I might add. You used to visit him on the flimsiest pretext, with the sole intention of helping him out.
Sir David Of the wine, she means of course, and not this world.
Hamilton His will was a legal nicety, a joy to read and a *pleasure* to administer.
Sir David How right you are. He wrote it on the back of an unpaid parking ticket and had it witnessed by a meter maid. The litigation over it lasted three years after which there was only enough left to pay the parking fine.
Lady Metcalfe Without him your career might never have taken off. Don't forget the Halford murders.
Sir David (*remembering*) Cardiff, Assizes. It was the first time I had appeared professionally in the city of my birth. My mother sat in the gallery. I never uttered a word, but every time I passed a piece of paper to Sir Danvers, she applauded.
Pierson I've never appeared in Cardiff.
Sir David (*in a Welsh accent*) There's nothing quite like Cardiff and the outlaying parts of South Wales—and no-one can out *lie* parts of South Wales. It was my first case as a junior and I'll never forget . . . the swearing in of the jury—a jury of cultured, intelligent, sensitive Welshmen. The Clerk of the Court told the jurors to take their usual place and they all climbed into the dock. The first one taking the oath looked at the card and said "I swear by Almighty God that I will well and truly try the severe issues joined between our *Soviet* Lady the Queen"—and the third one said "No, no my lord, no, I'm not having this, it's not right I should be on a jury. I'm not fit to serve on a jury", he says. "I'm as deaf as a post", he says, and then he opened his jacket and hanging on his waistcoat pocket was what looked like a pre-war wireless set with a wire leading to his left ear and he began to turn the knobs and it oscillated and whistled, and he said, "You can see the position is this, my lord, I'm as deaf as a post and if I can't hear the evidence, how can I hope to do justice according to law?"

The learned judge trying the case leaned down to the Clerk of the Court and said, "What did he say, Robinson?"

Hamilton I like to believe the Campbell case on which I instructed you was your breakthrough to success. Alice Campbell. You remember her?

Sir David I do indeed. Theft, adultery, perjury, blackmail and attempted murder. She certainly complied with the late Lord Russell's dictum that the Ten Commandments should be treated like an exam paper—only five need to be attempted.

Hamilton Your defence of her launched what has turned out to be a remarkable career. (*To Lady Metcalfe*) Your husband has no peer at the criminal bar.

Lady Metcalfe No, I don't know. It never pays to underestimate Anthony Blair-Booth.

Sir David Rubbish. You can't underestimate Anthony Blair-Booth.

Lady Metcalfe To quote *The Times* one of Britain's most distinguished advocates?

Sir David My darling, Harrow, Christchurch and Lincoln's Inn are incapable of producing anyone who might be described as distinguished.

Lady Metcalfe Whereas Cardiff Grammar School, Jesus College and the Inner Temple might?

Sir David Precisely, my dear, and what's more Blair-Booth's father was an estate agent whereas my old pater was in finance.

Lady Metcalfe Darling, you're not trying to convince a jury now. Anthony Blair-Booth's father was a senior partner with Knight, Frank and Rutley while your old dad was a counter clerk in the Swansea Building Society.

Sir David And what's more his father left him a small fortune, whereas all mine left to me was my mother. Dying fathers should make provision for their wives in their wills. They should leave them to someone else.

Lady Metcalfe You adore your mother. Where do you think all that so-called oratory comes from. And what's more, she's the only person who shares your own high opinion of yourself. Anyway, I still believe this trial will prove to be a fair contest between equals.

Sir David Nonsense ... the odds are totally loaded against me. We know my client was having an affair with the man. We know her fingerprints were on the murder weapon. We know——

Lady Metcalfe (*interrupting*) That you give us this "against overwhelming odds routine" before every trial only so that it will appear all the more impressive when you win.

Sir David Whose side are you on?

Lady Metcalfe In any case, do you really believe a jury will send a beautiful woman to jail for the rest of her life?

Sir David Not if I can get twelve men on the jury, they won't.

Hamilton Blair-Booth is far too cunning to let you get away with that.

Sir David I need a dozen over-sexed, middle-aged sales reps whose wives don't understand them. I think I'll get her to repeat her telephone number a few times during cross-examination.

Hamilton I haven't fully recovered from the advice you gave her when she asked, "How shall I give my evidence?"

Lady Metcalfe What did you say, David?

Sir David (*in a Welsh accent*) Well my dear, I said, just let it come out as though it were the truth.

Pierson I think her confidence will impress a jury. Though you can never be sure how a witness will turn out once they're in the box. What is it you always say, David? "Beware of the most confident, they often have the most to hide."

Mrs Rogers enters

Mrs Rogers Excuse me, my lady. Dinner is almost ready. If you'd just like to check.

Sir David About time too, I'm famished.

Lady Metcalfe Then be thankful for Mrs Rogers, because without her, you wouldn't have anything.

She joins Mrs Rogers at the door. They exit to the dining-room

Sir David moves towards the drinks table

Sir David Let me refill your glasses . . .

Hamilton refuses

Robert?

He accepts. Hamilton joins Sir David

Hamilton How is she, David?

Sir David No better, I'm afraid. She can still rise to the big occasion, like dinner tonight, but she soon pays for it, poor darling. I'm sorry to say that the latest reports give little room for hope. They go on taking tests. Pills help kill the pain for a time, but the relapses become more and more frequent. They talk about a wonder-cure some time in the future. But I fear—we both know—that the future is beginning to run out.

Hamilton (*deeply upset*) I'm so dreadfully sorry. I've never really been very good with words, but . . . I'm so sorry.

Sir David Let's not talk about it, tonight. There's nothing any of us can do. And even to think about it is . . . well, doesn't help. So . . .

Hamilton I'm sorry. I didn't mean to . . .

Sir David No, of course not. And I appreciate—we both do—your concern. Thank you, Lionel.

Pierson Good heavens. I had no idea you had a first name, Mr Hamilton.

Sir David Don't get cheeky, young man. Only High Court Judges, elderly QCs and the Chairman of the Bar Council—occasionally—can be familiar with Mr Hamilton.

Hamilton Though, I may make an exception of you, Pierson—but not until you're a QC.

Sir David Are you expecting any bombshells from Blair-Booth, tomorrow, Lionel?

Hamilton None that I'm aware of, not that he would ever let on, anyway. He is always so uncooperative especially when he's up against you.

Pierson Why does he take every case so personally?

Sir David Quite simple, really. I was a year behind him at Oxford, and he couldn't stand the fact that a Grammar School boy arrived and took from him both the things he assumed were his by right.

Pierson What do you mean?

Sir David Lionel has known for some time, but Blair-Booth proposed to Millicent the summer before I arrived at Oxford.

Pierson Oh. I had no idea. And of course, you pipped him for the Presidency of the Union.

Sir David A minor prize compared with Millie.

Hamilton A judgement with which I am fully able to concur.

Sir David I couldn't have put it more romantically myself.

Pierson Do you think Blair-Booth holds a party before the trial?

Sir David Certainly not.

Pierson How can you be so sure?

Sir David Because if he did, he'd have to subpoena the guests.

Lady Metcalfe enters, closing the doors behind her

Hamilton I'm sure you're right.

Lady Metcalfe Right about what, Lionel?

Sir David (*before anyone can answer*) Dylan Thomas.

Lady Metcalfe Oh, not him again. You know, just because David was born in Bridgend and heard the bard lecture once, he's totally obsessed.

Sir David Slander, and reliable witnesses to clear my name. I not only attended one of his lectures, but I got drunk with the great man afterwards. (*In a Welsh accent*) "Time passes. Listen. Time passes. Come closer now. Only you can hear the houses sleeping in the streets in the slow deep salt and silent black, bandaged night. Only you can see, in the blinded bedrooms, the coms. And petticoats over the chairs, the jugs and basins, the glasses of teeth, Thou Shalt Not on the wall, and the yellowing dickybird-watching pictures of the dead. Only you can hear and see, behind the eyes of the sleepers, the movements and countries and mazes and colours and dismays and rainbows and tunes and wishes and flight and fall and despairs and big seas of their dreams. From where you are, you can hear their dreams."

Mrs Rogers enters and interrupts at his peak

Mrs Rogers Dinner is served, my lady.

The telephone starts to ring. Mrs Rogers moves towards it, but is halted by Sir David

Sir David It's all right. (*To his wife*) You go in. I'll deal with it. (*Indicating the wine tray*) Robert, take this with you. (*He picks up the phone*) Hello?

Hamilton gallantly offers his arm to Lady Metcalfe, who takes it. They exit into the dining-room, followed—separately—by Mrs Rogers and Pierson

(*Into the telephone*) Yes. . . . Speaking. Who is it? Holbrook? Did you get the shares? (*He listens*) Good. (*He listens again*) The bid will be announced on Thursday. My source is impeccable. Naturally, I shall want you to sell within the account. (*He listens*) That gives you a clear ten days and when your senior partner returns from his holiday, I'm sure he will acknowledge your wise decision. . . . Yes, I'm aware that I've had a rather bad run lately, but I'm about to make it up . . . I have never let you down in the past, have I? (*He listens*) The sum is larger this time because the source is even more reliable. I don't see how anyone could describe me as an insider.

The dining-room door opens and Lady Metcalfe looks in, enquiring

I'll talk to you on Thursday. Good-night. (*He slams the phone down*)

Sir David and Lady Metcalfe exit to the dining-room

The Lights fade and the curtain falls

Voice-over 1

Sir David Mr Hamilton, there is no suggestion, is there, that I was at any time financially embarrassed?
Hamilton Not to my knowledge, Sir David.
Sir David Or that I was in any particular need of money?
Hamilton No sir. You have received for many years a most healthy income from the Bar, where your services were greatly sought.
Sir David How long have you known my wife and myself?
Hamilton I have served you both for twenty years.
Sir David And what was your opinion of our relationship?
Hamilton Above reproach. One could only admire, indeed envy, you both.

The voice-over ends

Scene 2

Later that evening

Hamilton, Pierson and Sir David are entering. Sir David carries a tray with four cups of coffee and a glass of brandy, Pierson a glass of port

Hamilton An appropriate choice for the trial of Mrs Cutts; the finest rare beef.
Pierson Yes, but did you notice how Millie poured the blood back into the gravy?
Sir David Simply destroying the evidence, my boy.
Hamilton And no doubt, that was the reason for producing that irresistible chocolate gâteau in the shape of a pair of scissors.
Pierson But why the hazelnut sauce?
Sir David The rust, you fool, the rust. My God, he's so slow, he reminds me of Geoffrey Boycott.

Lady Metcalfe enters

Lady Metcalfe Not as slow as you were over Mr Justice Fanshawe, QC.
Sir David Dear old Gerald.

Lady Metcalfe Dear old Gerald? Did you ever come across Gerald Fanshawe, Robert?

Pierson Only by reputation.

Lady Metcalfe He died, a few years ago, on the opening day of the Lords
Test Match against Australia.

Pierson Good Lord, were we that bad?

Lady Metcalfe What was bad was that no-one noticed until close-of-play at
six-thirty!

Pierson Wasn't it Gerald Fanshawe who took a visiting African chief to the
Lords Test Match and was rather taken aback when he overheard the
chief say in the Long Room afterwards, that he was surprised to see the
English still practise Black Magic?

Sir David Black Magic. What did Gerald have to say about that?

Pierson He demanded an explanation. "Well," said the chief, "You take me
to a wide open space surrounded by thousands of people, watching
twenty-two men all dressed in tribal white. Then the tallest man hurls a
ceremonial ball at a man with a stick and it hits him on the leg. 'Owsat!'
shout all the others on the field. Then a witch doctor in a long white coat
points his finger to the sky—and it rains for five days."

Hamilton You won't get much time for watching test matches this year.

Sir David I don't see why not. The better class of criminal always take five
days off for the Lords Test, so why shouldn't I?

Pierson But as Chairman of the Bar Council, David, you should be making
radical changes.

Sir David I certainly hope so. I intend to see that there are more women
elected to the Bar Council in the hope that, when I retire, we shall be able
to appoint the first woman chairman.

Hamilton Perish the thought. It's bad enough having women in our
profession, without having one as Chairman of the Bar Council. Forgive
me for criticizing your sex, dear lady, but I fear women barristers can only
bring the law into disrepute.

Lady Metcalfe With whom?

Hamilton The criminals, of course.

Sir David Lionel's quite right. The criminal classes are deeply conservative
in these matters. No hardened criminal will ever request a woman to
defend him. Well, hardly ever.

Hamilton None of my partners would ever consider instructing a woman.

Lady Metcalfe Shame on them, Lionel. We must all be willing to accept
that change is inevitable.

Sir David Yes, but I fear in our profession, they do like to change slowly.

Hamilton Quite. And now they are beginning to turn up everywhere. They
are not the same as us, my dear.

Lady Metcalfe (*drily*) You'd noticed?

Hamilton I suppose I'm old-fashioned, but I must confess, I am appalled
whenever a woman is appointed to the bench.

Sir David Oh, come on, that has to happen ... it's no more than common
sense and, anyway, judges dress up like transvestites and often behave like
old women.

Lady Metcalfe Agreed. In fact we need a lot more women judges. After all, we do have a woman Prime Minister.

Hamilton Don't remind me. Heavens, look at the time, I must be off.

Lady Metcalfe Are you going so soon?

Hamilton We have an early consultation with dear Mrs Cutts——

Lady Metcalfe Cutts! That's an unfortunate name for a Scissor Stabber.

Sir David She stabbed no-one, it was all a dreadful mistake.

Sir David exits to the hall

Hamilton—at nine o'clock sharp, so I fear I must leave you. Another wonderful dinner, dear lady. One almost looks forward to a good murder, in anticipation. (*He kisses her hand*) Perhaps, when Sir David has won the Beverley Cutts case, you might care to visit my humble abode for a meal.

Sir David enters with Hamilton's coat

Lady Metcalfe How can we be certain he's going to win the case, with that clever Anthony Blair-Booth against him?

Sir David Ha, ha. A conspiracy?

Lady Metcalfe And then I wouldn't be able to accept your kind invitation.

Sir David Are you inviting Millie to dine *à deux*, Lionel?

Hamilton Oh, no, you misunderstand, the invitation was for you both.

Sir David helps him on with his coat which is exactly the same make as the one Sir David wore when he first came in

Are you sure that's mine, David?

Sir David In the words of the head porter of Jesus College, Oxford, on being asked the same question by Lord Nuffield ... (*He imitates*) "I couldn't be sure it's yours, sir, but it's certainly the one you came in."

Hamilton Good-night, Millicent ... and thank you again ...

Lady Metcalfe Good-night, Lionel.

Hamilton Good-night, dear boy.

Sir David escorts Hamilton to the hall, to the front door

Pierson He's remarkable old Hamilton, isn't he? Pretends to be out of touch, but underneath, a first-class legal mind, years of experience sprinkled with a great deal of common sense.

Lady Metcalfe A sad man, though, I sometimes think. Lonely.

Pierson He should have married someone like you ... (*He pecks her on the cheek*) Sir David is very lucky.

The front door slams, off

Lady Metcalfe And you, young man, are more of an old ham than he is.

Sir David comes into the room again

Sir David Who's talking about me? Trying to pick up my wife again?

Pierson Whenever I get the chance. Well, now we've been caught out, I'd better slink off. I suppose. A ham, you say? Well, after fifteen years as his junior, it's hardly surprising.

Sir David You should have taken me as a warning, not as an example. You're not really going, Robert? Stay and have a nightcap. Two nightcaps?

Pierson No, I must be off.

Lady Metcalfe Must you?

Pierson (*to Sir David*) Why do people say "must you?" when what they really mean is "you must". I'll see you at the Bailey in the morning, David.

Sir David Will you? (*Quickly*) No, what I mean is—you will. Nine sharp. Because one thing is certain, Lionel will be on time.

Pierson Nine sharp—don't stay up too late. And don't underestimate Blair-Booth.

Sir David Is this my junior? Or my mentor?

Pierson It's been a lovely evening, Millie and a splendid meal, as always. Thanks.

Lady Metcalfe Good-night.

Sir David exits to the hall with Pierson

While he is seeing him off, Lady Metcalfe rises, suffers a painful attack and collapses in the chair, right. The front door slams, off

Sir David returns

Sir David A triumph, my darling. Are you all right?

Lady Metcalfe Fine. Was Lionel hinting when he talked about Robert taking silk?

Sir David Yes, this year, would be my guess. Oh, dear, I don't relish the prospect. I shall miss him as my junior.

Lady Metcalfe Perhaps, it's time you gave up, and became a curmudgeonly old judge.

Sir David That's a thought.

Lady Metcalfe And then you can marry a rich widow and——

Sir David Please don't.

Lady Metcalfe We have to think about it.

Sir David But it's still some time in the future. Dr Weeden said himself you'd be around for years.

Lady Metcalfe But did you look into the good doctor's eyes when he said it? David—I did. It's no use fooling ourselves, we're talking of months at best. I *know*.

Sir David Oh, Millie. I wish it were me and not you. I wish I could make that gift to you.

Lady Metcalfe Even if you could, I wouldn't accept it. You'll go on forever. You'll make a century. And I want you to enjoy every moment of it.

Sir David Not without you, Millie.

Lady Metcalfe Remember me, but only to recall the good times. Do you know, when I first met you, you were without exception the most arrogant, conceited, exciting man I'd ever come across.

Sir David (*in a Welsh accent*) And I haven't changed.

Lady Metcalfe No, except now you make me laugh even more.

Mrs Rogers enters, carrying a tray with a glass of water and gets the pills from the drawer in the phone table

Sir David (*irritated*) Can't you knock?

Mrs Rogers You must take your once-a-week pill tonight, my lady.

Sir David That woman has a gift for timing that Woody Allen would be proud of.

Lady Metcalfe Thank you, Mrs Rogers. That will be all for now. (*Brightly*) Good-night.

Mrs Rogers Good-night, my lady.

Mrs Rogers exits

Sir David Oh . . . er . . . good-night, Mrs Rogers. (*But she has already gone*)

Lady Metcalfe You really should be more considerate towards her. Try some of that charm you put to such good use with juries.

Sir David Why should I bother when the fact is that ever since her husband walked out on her she's taken it out on me.

Lady Metcalfe Perhaps she thinks you might do the same thing to me one day.

Sir David stares for a second at Lady Metcalfe and then gives her the pills

Thank you.

Sir David crosses to L *and puts the lamps off*

I wish we'd been able to have children, then at least . . .

Sir David Perhaps, if you had married Anthony Blair-Booth . . .

Lady Metcalfe Good heavens, no. Even when he proposed, he did it through instructing solicitors. No, I ended up with the right man.

Sir David (*in a Welsh accent*) "I am a draper mad with love. I love you more than all the flannelette and calico, candlewick, dimity, crash and merino, tussore, cretonne, crepon, muslin, poplin, ticking and twill in the whole Cloth Hall of the world. I have come to take you away to my Emporium on the hill, where the change hums on wires. (*He helps Lady Metcalfe to rise*) Throw away your little bedsocks and your Welsh wool knitted jacket, (*they move to the stairs*) I will warm the sheets like an electric toaster, I will lie by your side like the Sunday roast." (*He turns off the wall switches*)

Lady Metcalfe "I will knit you a wallet of forget-me-not blue, for the money to be comfy. I will warm your heart by the fire so that you can slip it under your vest when the shop is closed." David . . .

They embrace as the Lights fade

Voice-over 2

Sir David Is it possible that despite having worked for my wife for some considerable time you misunderstood the relationship between us?

Mrs Rogers What do you mean?

Sir David Exactly what I say.

Judge (*intervening*) Mrs Rogers, do you think Sir David and Lady Metcalfe might have got on well together, but you didn't fully appreciate their relationship?

Mrs Rogers No, my lord, that is not possible. I watched them together over many years. Lady Metcalfe was a very charming woman, but Sir David was always drunk and shouting at both of us.

Sir David I think what Mrs Rogers is trying to tell the court, my lord, is that she doesn't like me.

Mrs Rogers No I don't.

Sir David No, in fact, you don't have a good word to say for me—do you?

Mrs Rogers If there was anything good to say, I would be happy to tell the Judge.

Sir David So you're only interested in saying harmful things.

Mrs Rogers No. I didn't say that. You're trying to put words into my mouth like you do with everybody. I only want the truth to come out.

The voice-over ends

SCENE 3

A week later, the evening of 23rd March

Lady Metcalfe is on the phone

Lady Metcalfe A foregone conclusion? Well, let's hope so. (*She listens*) Yes, do tell me . . .

Mrs Rogers enters

(*Covering the phone*) Just clear away, Mrs Rogers . . . and I'd love a cup of coffee.

Mrs Rogers Will Sir David be eating at home tonight?

Lady Metcalfe I doubt it. It's the last day of the Scissors Stabber trial and the jury are still out, so I've really no idea when he will be home.

Mrs Rogers clears away the tray and exits

(*Into the phone*) Absolutely, my dear. . . . Of course . . . I'll tell him the moment he arrives . . .

Sir David enters

(*To Sir David*) "Has God come home?"

Sir David Who is it?

Lady Metcalfe Your mother.

Sir David shakes his head

(*Into the phone*) But you know what he's like, it might be hours before he gets back . . . especially while he is waiting for a verdict. . . . Celebrating perhaps . . . (*she looks at Sir David*) . . . or not, as the case may be. . . . No, I'm fine. . . . Really, I promise. . . . Of course, I will call you the moment he comes in. . . . All right, my dear, thank you . . . much love. . . . Yes, goodbye . . .

Sir David You should have a tape made on one of those ansaphone contraptions. "My dear . . . of course, I'll let him know . . . the moment he comes in . . . I realize David is the most wonderful man in the world, and how lucky I am . . . my dear, of course I'll let him know . . ."
Lady Metcalfe She's an old lady, and she doesn't see enough of you.
Sir David I don't see enough of *you*.
Lady Metcalfe All right, I give in. I wasn't going to ask until you told me— but I can't bear the suspense any longer.
Sir David Something you wanted to know?
Lady Metcalfe Was Mrs Cutts guilty, or not guilty?
Sir David That, my dear, is two questions, only one of which was decided by the jury.
Lady Metcalfe Stop being infuriating, David. I'm waiting.

Sir David clears his throat

Sir David Members of the jury, I stand before you today——
Lady Metcalfe Darling. I don't have to listen to the whole of your closing speech, do I?
Sir David Actually, I was going to begin with my opening speech.
Lady Metcalfe Perhaps, we could just have the edited highlights?
Sir David What? How dare you.

Mrs Rogers enters with Lady Metcalfe's coffee and hears him shouting

Mrs Rogers Your coffee. My lady.
Lady Metcalfe (*to Sir David*) Would you like some? (*She sees he would not*) Thank you, Mrs Rogers.

Mrs Rogers exits

Sir David Very well, the peroration. Members of the jury, you may feel that the Crown, in presenting its case, has failed dismally as it was conceived in chaos and conducted in confusion.
Lady Metcalfe That was very rude, David. What on earth must Anthony Blair-Booth have thought of you?
Sir David Not a lot, probably. Am I to expect a string of mindless interruptions, Millie? You're worse than a hostile witness. Where was I?
Lady Metcalfe In confusion.
Sir David The Crown's dismal failure to produce any evidence which could stand up to cross-examination . . . indeed, evidence which when looked at carefully, proved to be nothing more than threads and patches, flimsy and fanciful.
Lady Metcalfe Surely, Anthony Blair-Booth protested?
Sir David No, my dear. Unlike you, he knows you do *not* interrupt defence counsel's closing speech. Where was I?
Lady Metcalfe Flimsy and fanciful.
Sir David In the extreme. Evidence which under cross-examination proved to be nothing more than hearsay—second- and sometimes even third-hand. Evidence on which you, members of the jury, are being asked to rely, to decide the fate of the defendant, Beverley Cutts.

Sir David gestures dramatically to where Lady Metcalfe sits. Lady Metcalfe sits up to assume the persona of Beverley Cutts. Sir David points to Lady Metcalfe

Is it possible that this slight, gentle lady could have overpowered a six foot, thirteen stone man, and plunged a pair of scissors into him—not once—but seven times.

Lady Metcalfe (*herself*) He could have been asleep.

Sir David Millie!

Sir David gestures to Lady Metcalfe again who dutifully returns to the role of Beverley Cutts

The defendant lady never tried to hid the fact that she had sexual intercourse with the man Kendrick . . . but which of you on this jury would send a young woman to gaol for the rest of her life . . . on the sole charge that she had committed adultery.

Lady Metcalfe (*briskly, herself again*) But that wasn't the sole charge——

Sir David Millie! (*He picks up the napkin from the sofa and throws it at her*) I submit to you that such evidence is no basis on which to build a case against the defendant—and certainly no basis for a conviction for murder. *You* must be certain *beyond reasonable doubt* that she is a bloody murderess. I repeat, *certain* that this frail pitiful woman thrust those scissors again and again . . . and again and again into the body of that huge man.

Lady Metcalfe Huge! (*She sighs*) Not bad. Then what?

Sir David Then Mr Justice Trubshaw summed up, posing the question of who did commit the murder, if Mrs Cutts didn't.

Lady Metcalfe Good point.

Sir David He also felt that my client's explanation for her fingerprints being on the scissors was not altogether convincing. He praised Blair-Booth for his thoroughness in prosecution and me for my boldness in defence—whatever that meant. I wasn't sure. And then the jury retired.

Lady Metcalfe (*after a pause*) Well, come on?

Sir David After three hours they sent a note up saying they couldn't agree.

Lady Metcalfe And?

Sir David In the end, by a majority verdict of ten to two—Mrs Cutts was found . . . (*pause*) . . . Not Guilty.

Lady Metcalfe So, she was innocent.

Sir David Millie, have you been listening to one word I've said? The jury were convinced by the presentation of the defence, not by her case.

Lady Metcalfe So, what will happen to Mrs Cutts now?

Sir David Who knows? She left the court in a flood of tears, refusing to utter a syllable to the Press.

Lady Metcalfe Well, that shows a certain sensitivity.

Sir David Sensitivity be damned. I'm told she's sold her exclusive life story to *The People* for fifty thousand quid—in which, I understand, she promises to reveal who did murder her lover.

Lady Metcalfe That could prove embarrassing.

Sir David Only for Blair-Booth. When she admits she did it. I must remember to pick up a copy on Sunday.

Lady Metcalfe How did Anthony take the verdict?

Sir David Sulked, and then marched out of the court in a huff. He's such a bad loser despite having had a lot of practice at it.

Lady Metcalfe And you are always so unsympathetic to the poor man.

Sir David Not at all. He brings it on himself, self-satisfied——

Lady Metcalfe David. Have you no regard for Anthony?

Sir David Regard for Anthony? I have as much regard for Blair-Booth as a chicken does for Colonel Sanders. Come on, let's have a decent drink to celebrate.

Lady Metcalfe All right. Have you had time to eat?

Sir David Sort of: upstairs in the Bailey. Though I confess I could do with a decent bottle of wine. The Bailey has taken proof of innocence to an extreme. Ever since those obscenity trials, the only wine you can purchase is Blue Nun.

Lady Metcalfe Right, the Mouton Rothschild, then.

Sir David No, we're down to the last case.

Lady Metcalfe But it's a celebration. And in any case, I've already decanted a bottle.

Sir David You wicked woman, you always knew I'd win, didn't you?

The phone rings. Lady Metcalfe answers it

Lady Metcalfe Hello? ... Yes, it is. (*To Sir David*) It's a Mr Holbrook.

Sir David Holbrook?

Lady Metcalfe He says it's important.

Sir David All right, I'll take it.

Lady Metcalfe While you're chatting I'll ask Mrs Rogers to fetch the wine.

Lady Metcalfe exits

Sir David moves to the phone

Sir David Holbrook, yes. (*He listens*) Well, you'll have to sell them by close of business tomorrow. ... Yes, but how was I to know the Government were going to send the Inspectors in. Sell the damn things. Don't worry about the shortfall. (*Looking towards the door*) I will soon be able to cover it. ...

Mrs Rogers enters carrying the wine

Don't push me. Your senior partner remains one of my closest friends. (*He glances upwards and sees Mrs Rogers*) Get out. You stupid woman. Get out!

Mrs Rogers runs out

Sir David speaks into the phone again, but looks towards the door through which Lady Metcalfe exited

Call me tomorrow at my chambers. I will have secured the money by then. (*He slams down the phone*)

As he does so, Lady Metcalfe comes in

Lady Metcalfe David, *why* did you shout at Mrs Rogers?

Sir David She listens to conversations that are none of her business.
Lady Metcalfe That's nonsense. She wouldn't begin to understand your private conversations, and you know it. She couldn't be more honest and loyal.
Sir David Loyal to you, perhaps.
Lady Metcalfe I wish you'd apologize to her . . . though I know you won't . . . I'll have to do it for you. Was it Mr Holbrook who upset you?
Sir David No, no.
Lady Metcalfe Who is he? A client?
Sir David No . . . yes, a client. I told him to call me tomorrow in chambers.
Lady Metcalfe I'm sorry, I'd have put him off if I'd known. But he said it was important.
Sir David Yes, I know. But importance is relative, isn't it? For me, you see, only *you* are important. (*Offering her a glass of wine*) You will join me?
Lady Metcalfe (*accepting*) As it's a special occasion. (*She raises her glass*) Congratulations, David, I shouldn't say it, since everyone else does anyway, but it must have been a triumph.
Sir David In some ways.
Lady Metcalfe What's this . . . a confession? You mean you're fallible?
Sir David I make the occasional howler.
Lady Metcalfe Tell. Please. Do. Problem, David?

They stare at each other for a moment as if he is about to admit to something

Mrs Rogers enters

Mrs Rogers Would you like some more coffee, my lady?
Lady Metcalfe No, thank you.

Mrs Rogers exits

Sir David Please note she didn't offer to bring *me* a cup of coffee.
Lady Metcalfe She is well aware of your *drinking* habits, and in any case, the way you treat her, who can blame the woman? She's terrified of you.
Sir David Oh—I'd explain to her about barks and bites if I thought she would understand . . .
Lady Metcalfe She certainly sees you as some sort of wild dog. And I've lost enough servants over the years because of your temper.
Sir David I know, but I am mellowing now, hadn't you noticed? And I promise I'll never bark at her again.
Lady Metcalfe Good. Because she has a completely distorted view of you . . . which is a pity because you're a darling, really.
Sir David I am? You're absolutely right. But then you have such wonderful judgement and impeccable taste. You always did. That's why I married you. Let's have another drink.
Lady Metcalfe Be careful or you'll have to open another bottle. You're almost out.
Sir David (*in a Welsh accent*) So long as it's just you and me, let's finish off the case.
Lady Metcalfe No. Save it. Drink it in memory of me.
Sir David Millie . . .

Lady Metcalfe I only meant . . . you know . . . it was something we shared . . . something you could look back on.

Sir David I wouldn't need this to assist me.

Lady Metcalfe I know, but it's a whim. Let me give instructions for the last few bottles to be hidden.

Sir David Certainly not and in any case, it wouldn't be long before I found them.

Lady Metcalfe So.

Sir David I would polish them off when you weren't looking.

Lady Metcalfe Then I would have you arrested for theft.

Sir David Me. Ah. You'd have a job to prove that.

Lady Metcalfe Why?

Sir David Because before the case ever came to court, I would have destroyed the evidence.

Lady Metcalfe That's cheating. I would inform the prosecuting counsel of the facts.

Sir David Anthony Blustering Blair-Booth, QC, no doubt.

Lady Metcalfe Of course. A most distinguished advocate.

Sir David Pompous twit.

Lady Metcalfe And I would personally enter the witness box. "Drunk, my lord, always drunk, the whole of our married life."

Sir David (*joining in*) A vicious, prejudiced wife who always lacked compassion and understanding, driving her mild, tolerant husband to the solace of the bottle.

Lady Metcalfe An uncontrollable drunk, knowing that alcohol was destroying his brain, but too . . . befuddled . . . to stop it . . . his secret fear that one day, his *younger* rival, would confront and humiliate him . . .

Sir David Younger . . . you will live to regret those words, woman . . . (*He takes up bottle of wine and raises it threateningly*)

Lady Metcalfe No. Don't hit me. Not again. I can't take any more. (*Then as herself, quietly*) Well, not with the Mouton Rothschild anyway . . .

Sir David (*lowering the bottle*) I wouldn't waste it on you, woman. I shall look for a non-vintage bottle.

Lady Metcalfe I confess . . .

Sir David places a handkerchief on his head and a pair of hornrim glasses on his nose taking up the pose of a judge

Sir David Lady Millicent Metcalfe, you have been found guilty of a most heinous crime by twelve good men——

Lady Metcalfe No good women on the jury, I note.

Sir David —of falsely accusing, and constantly nagging, the defendant, Sir David Metcalfe, who for twenty-eight years has been a lovable, sweet-tempered, gentle and attentive husband. Have you anything to say before I pass sentence?

Lady Metcalfe Have mercy . . . please.

Sir David I have no choice in the matter. . . I must pass the maximum sentence the law allows . . . I sentence you to fifteen years . . . more . . . with Sir David Metcalfe.

Lady Metcalfe I appeal.
Sir David Appeal dismissed.
Lady Metcalfe Oh, David . . .
Sir David Why do the young always assume that love is their prerogative?
Lady Metcalfe Stop being a silly sentimental old thing . . . and let's finish off the bottle.
Sir David Good idea. Millie . . . are you all right . . . ?
Lady Metcalfe (*leaning back*) Yes, I'm fine . . . just keep me laughing . . . it does help . . .

There is a knock and Mrs Rogers enters

Sir David Good heavens, discretion at last. You see, persevere and the message will always get through.
Lady Metcalfe What is it, Mrs Rogers?
Mrs Rogers You must take your once-a-week pill tonight, my lady. (*She takes the pill bottles from the phone table drawer*)
Lady Metcalfe Oh, yes. . . thank you.
Sir David Another black mark for the master . . . no hot-water bottle on his side of the bed tonight.

Mrs Rogers gives Lady Metcalfe both pill bottles and a glass of water as Sir David creeps up behind her

Mrs Rogers Good-night, my lady.
Lady Metcalfe Good-night, Mrs Rogers.
Sir David (*in a loud Welsh voice*) Isn't life a terrible thing, thank God.

Mrs Rogers runs out

Lady Metcalfe You must remember that her memories of married life are not all that happy. And it can't be any fun being all alone.
Sir David (*in a Welsh accent*) "Alone until she dies, Bessie Bighead, hired help, born in the workhouse, smelling of the cowshed, snores bass and gruff on a couch of straw in a loft in Salt Lake Farm and picks a posy of daisies in Sunday Meadow to put on the grave of Gomer Owen, who kissed her once by the pigsty when she wasn't looking and never kissed her again, although she was looking all the time."

Lady Metcalfe starts to laugh, but it becomes too painful for her

Oh, Millie, I'm sorry. (*He comforts her*)
Lady Metcalfe I must be such a burden to you.
Sir David Never.
Lady Metcalfe David, I do worry about you. You're really not facing up to it. I want you to prepare, as I am. I don't want you to be an old codger at the club, like Benson. I really do hope you'll marry again; a nice widow, who can cook . . .
Sir David I will not listen to such stupidity, I do not want anyone else, Millie.
Lady Metcalfe You have a long life ahead of you, and so much still to achieve.

Sir David But no-one to share it with, Millie. To get the true value of happiness, you have to share it with someone you love. Whither shall I go and with whom shall I share my triumph, when the jury says: "Not Guilty"? There'll be no-one to grumble at about the biased old judge, no-one to whom I can expose the latest scandal in chambers. No-one who will be able to quote to me the next line of *Under Milk Wood* and still pretend she was hearing the words for the first time. No-one who will hold my hand and say, "whatever your excesses, I still love you".

Lady Metcalfe David . . .

Sir David I don't understand why you have to die, so don't ask me to be sensible, practical, or especially logical. I, too, want to "rage, rage against the dying of the light".

Lady Metcalfe But I don't want you to.

Sir David Can't you see what it will be like? Lionel clucking over me like a mother hen, Robert considerate as an elder son, my mother on the telephone endlessly, asking me how I am. But before long they'll be saying in the corridors of the Old Bailey: "He's not half the man he was". And then my secret will be out. Without you, I am less than half a man.

Lady Metcalfe David. I do love you. Will you help me up to bed.

Sir David I'm sorry I've been prattling on. I only thank God he let me have you at all, but I wonder what I did to anger him, that he couldn't have allowed me a little longer.

Lady Metcalfe It's a beautiful closing speech, but you must be sensible. Come on.

Sir David and Lady Metcalfe exit upstairs

Mrs Rogers enters from the kitchen, looks at the pill bottles on the table, puts the lights out

The Lights fade and the curtain falls

Voice-over 3

Blair-Booth And on the night in question, did Lady Metcalfe take her once-a-week pill, the red one?

Mrs Rogers Yes.

Blair-Booth And then a white sleeping pill?

Mrs Rogers Yes, sir. At about a quarter to ten.

Blair-Booth So she should not have taken another red pill for at least seven days?

Mrs Rogers Correct, sir. Those were the clear instructions I was given by Dr Weeden.

Blair-Booth I understand. And was Sir David in the room at the time?

Mrs Rogers Yes, he was.

Blair-Booth And did he witness what was going on?

Mrs Rogers Well, of course, he did. He was standing there wasn't he?

Blair-Booth But could Sir David have had any way of knowing which pill Lady Metcalfe was taking?

Mrs Rogers He must have known because when I give it to Lady Metcalfe I always describe it as the "once-a-week" pill so he knew all right.
Blair-Booth Always? So Sir David had heard the expression before?
Mrs Rogers Many times.

The voice-over ends

SCENE 4

Later that night

When the CURTAIN *rises Lady Metcalfe is seen lying on the floor between the sofa and the chair* L

After a few moments, Sir David is heard calling her name. He comes down the stairs into the drawing-room

Sir David (*switching on the lights*) Millie? Millie! (*He sees her*) Oh my God, Millie. Are you all right? What happened?
Lady Metcalfe I must have fallen.
Sir David I'm so sorry ... I had no idea you were up. Have you hurt yourself?
Lady Metcalfe I think I've only bruised my arm.
Sir David Why didn't you call me?
Lady Metcalfe You were so tired after the trial, I didn't want to disturb you.
Sir David That's silly.
Lady Metcalfe Anyway, as you're up now, I'd love a cup of tea.
Sir David Of course.
Lady Metcalfe If I could take just another pill I'll be fine.
Sir David Right ...

Sir David exits through the door which leads to the dining-room

Lady Metcalfe reaches out to the tray, on the table nearby, on which the pill-bottles stand, but the effort is too much for her. She gives up, obviously in great pain

(*Off; in a Welsh accent*) "In you reeled, my boy, as drunk as a deacon with a big wet bucket and a fish-frail full of stout and you looked at me and you said, 'God has come home!' you said."

Sir David enters

(*His normal voice*) I must have drunk more than I realized, or else I'd have heard you get up. I've put the kettle on.
Lady Metcalfe Thank you. David, I really hope it won't be too long now. I don't think I can take that much more. I find the pain harder to bear each day and I'm only trying to stay alive for you. But I need to ask you to let me go.
Sir David (*after a pause*) But you haven't even pruned the rose bed yet.

Lady Metcalfe (*trying to laugh*) You are so wonderful, David, and I do love you so much.
Sir David And I love you. (*Teasing*) I know, but I must leave you now.
Lady Metcalfe Why?
Sir David Because I hear the kettle boiling.

Sir David exits

Lady Metcalfe reaches for her pills and tries unsuccessfully to open the bottle

Sir David returns with a cup of tea

Couldn't find the Earl Grey but I discovered two tea bags ... you know, the ones those chimpanzees drink on television.
Lady Metcalfe Would you put the pill in the tea ... let it dissolve. I find it easier to take, that way.

She hands Sir David a bottle but the audience cannot see what colour the pills are

Mrs Rogers appears on the stairs

As she does to, Sir David has his back to her. He drops a pill into the tea, then returns to sit on the sofa next to Lady Metcalfe

Thank you ... (*She sips the tea*).
Sir David Millie ...
Lady Metcalfe No ... don't say anything more, David. I'm even too tired to laugh.

After Mrs Rogers has seen Lady Metcalfe sip the tea she exits upstairs

I'll be all right now, David ...
Sir David (*in a Welsh accent*) "I love you until death do us part and then we shall be together for ever and ever. A new parcel of ribbons has come from Carmarthen today, all the colours in the rainbow. I wish I could tie a ribbon in your hair a white one but it cannot be. I dreamed last night you were all dripping wet and you sat on my lap as the Reverend Jenkins went down the street. I see you got a mermaid in your lap he said and he lifted his hat. He is a proper Christian. Not like Cherry Owen who said you should have thrown her back he said ... My heart is in your bosom and yours is in mine. God be with you always Myfanwy Price and keep you lovely for me in His Heavenly Mansion." (*Softly, fearfully*) Millie ...? Oh Millie, please ... I'm sorry ... don't go yet. (*He continues to sob*)

The Lights fade to Black-out and the CURTAIN *falls*

Voice-over 4

Judge When you have weighed all the evidence as it has been presented to you, you will have to decide upon your verdict. It would be quite wrong for me to give you any idea as to what I think. The verdict is yours alone. Put out of your mind, anger, sympathy and all other emotions. If the evidence does not satisfy you beyond reasonable doubt you will bring a verdict of "Not Guilty", but on the other hand, if it does, your verdict, however unpalatable it may be—must be Guilty". I do not envy you your task but you must be resolute in your duty. When the Jury Bailiff has been sworn, you will retire to consider your verdict and in due course return and let me know how you find.

Clerk Will the defendant please rise. Will the foreman of the jury please stand. Mr Foreman, do you find the prisoner, Sir David Metcalfe, guilty or not guilty of murder?

The voice-over ends

SCENE 5

The living-room of the house at Wimbledon, about two weeks after the trial. It is 8 p.m. Sir David stands at the desk with his back to the audience

The clock chimes eight and on the fifth chime, the doorbell rings

Short pause, then Lionel Hamilton enters

Sir David It could only have been you, come in, Lionel. Bang on time.
Hamilton I'm glad you asked me. You've been living like a hermit since the verdict . . . phone off the hook, not answering letters . . . refusing even to see your closest friends.
Sir David Well now I've answered every letter and even written a few of my own, (*replacing the receiver*) the phone is back on the hook, and you've been invited round for a drink.
Hamilton (*seeing the bottle of red pills*) What are these doing here? (*He picks them up*)
Sir David The police returned them. I even had to sign for them. After all, they were Millie's and Millie left everything to me as Anthony Blair-Booth was only too keen to point out.
Hamilton Well, that's all over now. It was an unpleasant experience, but a satisfactory conclusion.

As Sir David hands him a glass

Let's drink a toast to that, at least. The Mouton Rothschild?
Sir David Yes, the very last bottle. Millie wanted me to save it for a special occasion. I've preferred to drink them—alone, with her in my thoughts—as a celebration of a different kind . . . but I wanted you to share the last one.
Hamilton Come . . . let's make this a happier occasion, David. I have an extraordinary case . . . of a boy who killed his mother—having dabbled in black magic, I have no doubt it will totally reinstate you at the Bar.
Sir David The Black Magic Murder Case. You almost tempt me, Lionel. But I can't return to the Bar. You see, it's no longer possible.
Hamilton Why not?
Sir David Because I did kill my wife.

Hamilton (*hesitating*) It was an accident, we all realize that.

Sir David No, Lionel. It was quite deliberate. That's what she wanted and I couldn't refuse her. I loved her too much.

Hamilton Oh God. I wish you hadn't told me. Why didn't you inform the police?

Sir David I'm afraid I didn't consider it was any of their business.

Hamilton But you're the Chairman of the Bar Council, of all people you cannot be above the law.

Sir David Well, on this occasion, I decided to be my own judge and jury. But I underestimated the honest Mrs Rogers and her chance to tell the truth as she saw it.

Hamilton You could have told the truth in court.

Sir David I did, by the standards of any politician. I don't consider I told any lies. Perhaps I was economical with the truth. What is truth asked jesting Pilate, and would not stay for answer. Do any of us ever know what the whole truth is? But I had intended to confess. I had even rehearsed the statement, and delivered at the right time, I know it would have convinced any jury.

Hamilton Then why didn't you?

Sir David Because quite suddenly I realized I was in a real fight: Blair-Booth was after me ... and very close to convincing that jury. If I had then told the whole truth—it would have looked like a pathetic apologia, an attempt to crawl out of my problems. If I had made that statement, the one I wanted to make—I had to make it with dignity. Don't leave your wine, Lionel. It is the last of the sixty-one. I suddenly understood, Lionel, that Blair-Booth and I were like two old antelopes locked in battle, for the last time. And for the first time I had allowed him to get the better of me.

Hamilton But why?

Sir David Because the person I was defending (*he points to himself*) didn't care about the outcome. I had lost the one thing I loved and even the pleasure of beating Blair-Booth couldn't bring Millie back. But I knew it would be my last case.

Hamilton It will certainly have been your last case. After this conversation, you can never hope to practise at the Bar again.

Sir David That's why I asked you over ... so that one person would know the truth—the whole truth—because you're the most honest man I know, Lionel, and I needed to explain to someone I trusted ... and respected ... I also needed someone to ... help me crack the last bottle—in memory of Millie. By the way, I've left you what remains of my cellar. It's not up to much now that the Mouton Rothschild has been finished, but I'm sure you'll appreciate what remains.

Hamilton (*rising*) What are you suggesting?

Sir David Shortly before you arrived—you're never late, old fellow, I took three of the Cyclotoxelix pills in my first glass of wine, which we know is fatal. Like Millie—the once-a-week pills, the red ones. She died very peacefully, Lionel.

Hamilton moves to the phone

No ... Lionel ... please. Don't. Please? Thank you, Lionel. It was good
of you to come, to be with me. I've written the necessary letters, cleared
up the estate. Everything's neat and tidy. I've left it all on my desk for you
to administer. The bulk of it is to go to the Chester Beattie Institute. I've
looked after my mother of course and I've even left a little something for
Mrs Rogers. I was delighted to read in *The Times* that Robert has become
a QC. He earned it. I'm only sorry that I'll never have the chance to chide
him from the judge's bench. Millie would have enjoyed that. She liked
Robert, God bless her. And she would have revelled in the Black Magic
Murder trial. I wonder what she would have prepared for dinner to
commemorate such an occasion. You were always good at guessing ...
Tell me, what would Millie have cooked for dinner the night before the
Black Magic Murder trial?

> "I see the boys of summer in their ruin
> And death shall have no dominion
> Rage, rage against the dying of the light
> I will go gentle into that good night."

*Hamilton crouches over Sir David. He reaches slowly for the phone and dials
999 as the Lights slowly fade and——*

                    —the CURTAIN *falls*

FURNITURE AND PROPERTY LIST

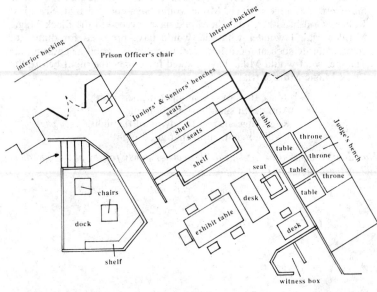

ACT I

On stage: Judge's bench. *On it:* red judge's book, pen, black book and papers, carafe
of water, glass. *On lower level:* Archbold

Table L of judge's bench. *On it:* Archbold, folders

Juniors' bench. *On it:* R *end* **(Pierson)**—tied-up brief, counsel book, carafe
of water, glass, Hamilton's file and pen, other dressing. L *end* **(Cole)**—
brief, counsel book, jury bundle, pen, carafe of water, glass

Seniors' bench. *On it:* L *end* **(Blair-Booth)**—high lectern, counsel book,
prosecution brief, carafe of water, glass, pen. R *end*—short lectern,
carafe of water, glass, pen, pencils, other dressing

Usher's table. *On it:* labelled pill bottle in brown envelope (exhibit 1), 2
carafes of water and glasses, Bible, oath card, usher's notes and buff
folders, pens, pencils, envelopes, etc.

Chairs

Clerk's table. *On it:* judge's jury bundle, pile of clear folders with one
marked "The Judge" on top, clerk's folder, pens, pencils, carafe of
water, glass, tea-towel set in black folder (in case of spillage of water)

Stenographer's table. *On it:* shorthand pad, pens, carafe of water, glass,
dictaphone, tissues, spare notepads, etc.

Swivel chair

Dock. *In it:* 2 chairs. On shelves: Archbold, carafe of water, glass, 2
   counsel books, brief, jury notes, pen, pencil, 3 clear pill bottles, 1
   containing blue pills, 1 green, the other red
   Witness box
   Chair for **Prison Officer**

Off stage: Bottle of white pills **(Cole)**
   Piece of paper **(Cole)**
   File **(Cole)**

Personal: **Travers:** police notebook, copy of death certificate
   Weeden: black notebook
   Blair-Booth: diary
   Prison Officer: black clip-board with witnesses' names
   Mrs Rogers: handbag with handkerchief

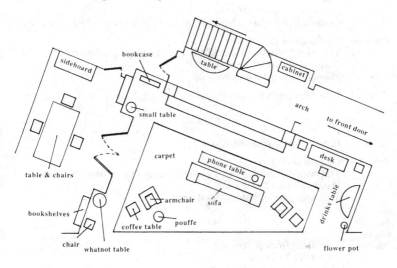

ACT II

SCENE 1

On stage: Drawing-room:
   Sofa. *On it:* cushions
   Long phone table. *On it:* telephone, framed photo of Lady Metcalfe, other
      dressing. *In drawer at* L *end:* 2 bottles of pills, 1 red, 1 white
   2 armchairs
   2 coffee tables with magazines underneath
   Built-in bookshelves with cupboards underneath. *On shelves:* books,
      carriage clock
   Chair
   Whatnot table. *On it:* lamp
   Bookcase. *On it:* ornaments
   Small table. *On it:* lamp, dressing

Writing desk. *On it:* writing materials, lamp
3 chairs around desk
Drinks table. *On it:* lamp, bottles of drink including whisky, water jug,
glasses. *Above it:* mirror
Tall flower pot
Carpet
Paintings on walls

Dining-room:
Sideboard. *On it:* dressing
Table dressed for dinner for 4
4 chairs
Paintings on walls

Hall:
Semi-circular table. *On it:* lamp, dressing
Glass-doored display cabinet. *On it:* lamp, ornaments. *Above it:* mirror

Off stage: Briefcase **(Sir David)**
Tray with 2 Mouton Rothschild bottles (1 empty), 1 full wine decanter, 4
wine glasses **(Mrs Rogers)**
Pierson's coat **(Mrs Rogers)**

Personal: **Lady Metcalfe:** wrist-watch

Scene 2

Strike: Plates, napkins from dining-table

Off stage: Glass of port **(Pierson)**
Tray with 4 cups of coffee, 1 glass of brandy **(Sir David)**
Hamilton's coat **(Sir David)**
Tray with glass of water **(Mrs Rogers)**

Scene 3

Strike: Everything from dining-table
Sir David's briefcase
Dirty glasses, coffee cups, trays

Set: Orthopaedic cushion, napkin on sofa
Invalid tray with bowl of soup, bread roll, dessert, cutlery
Telephone on back of sofa

Re-set: Bottle of red pills, bottle of white pills in drawer in phone table

Off stage: Briefcase, coat, hat **(Sir David)**
Small tray with cup of coffee **(Mrs Rogers)**
Tray with 2 wine glasses, empty Mouton Rothschild bottle, full wine
decanter **(Mrs Rogers)**
Small tray with glass of water **(Mrs Rogers)**

Personal: **Sir David:** handkerchief, hornrim glasses in pocket

Scene 4

Off stage: Cup of tea **(Sir David)**

SCENE 5

Strike: Orthopaedic cushion, napkin, coat, hat, briefcase, dirty cups and glasses, empty wine bottle, decanter, trays, white pill bottle

Set: Glass of wine, writing materials, addressed envelopes on desk
Full wine decanter and 3 glasses on drinks table
Telephone receiver off hook and on back of sofa

Re-set: Bottle of red pills to R end of phone table

Off stage: Tied-up brief document **(Hamilton)**

LIGHTING PLOT

Practical fittings required: ACT I—*nil*. ACT II—6 lamps, strip lights above paintings, 3-way switch on wall just inside drawing-room

2 interiors: a court and a drawing-room and adjoining hall and dining-room

ACT I

To open: General interior lighting

Cue 1	**Usher:** "Be upstanding in court." *Fade to black-out*	(Page 16)
Cue 2	When ready *Bring up general lighting*	(Page 16)
Cue 3	As **Sir David** crosses from the witness box to the dock *Fade to spot on* **Judge**	(Page 23)
Cue 4	**Judge:** "... let me know how you find." *Increase to general lighting*	(Page 24)
Cue 5	**Usher:** "... agreed upon their verdict." *Fade to spots on* **Clerk** *and* **Sir David**	(Page 24)
Cue 6	**Clerk:** "Will the defendant please rise." *Increase to general lighting*	(Page 24)
Cue 7	**Clerk:** "... guilty or not guilty of murder?" *Snap black-out*	(Page 24)

ACT II SCENE 1.   Evening

To open: General interior lighting on all areas, all practicals on

Cue 8	**Sir David** and **Lady Metcalfe** exit to the dining-room *Fade to black-out*	(Page 32)

ACT II SCENE 2.   Evening

To open General interior lighting on all areas, all practicals on

Cue 9	**Sir David** switches off lamp on desk *Snap off lamp on desk*	(Page 36)
Cue 10	**Sir David** switches off wall switches *Snap off all other lamps in lounge and covering lighting, leaving only hall and landing lit*	(Page 36)
Cue 11	**Lady Metcalfe:** "David ..." *They embrace* *Fade to black-out*	(Page 36)

ACT II SCENE 3.   Evening

To open: General interior lighting on all areas, all practicals on

Cue 12   **Mrs Rogers** switches out all the lights   (Page 44)
                Black-out

ACT II SCENE 4.   Night

To open: Lighting on hall and landing only

Cue 13   **Sir David** switches on wall switch   (Page 45)
                Snap up lamps on whatnot table and small table R

Cue 14   **Sir David:** "... I'm sorry ... don't go yet."   (Page 46)
                Fade to black-out

ACT II SCENE 5.   Evening

To open: General interior lighting on all areas, all practicals on

Cue 15   As **Hamilton** dials 999   (Page 49)
                Slow fade to black-out

EFFECTS PLOT

ACT I

No cues

ACT II